CEREBRUM: A DYSTOPIAN HORROR

Part One of the Sistema Series

ULTAN BANAN

Cover design by Ultan Banan © 2022

Editing by Paul @ Seminal Edits

ultanbanan.com

ISBN: 978-1-914147-19-7

CEREBRUM

I

Most people are familiar only with their own horror. I am intimate with all men's.

'Ready?'

'Sure.'

'Then let's do it.'

I heard the click of the button. My gut clenched. Then it came in a fury, like an ephemeral, lambent sideways rain, and a searing flash at the base of my skull right above the spine. I opened my eyes.

—You in?

I put my hand to my ear. 'Yeah. I think so.'

I was in darkness.

—Patching you in now.

The darkness shimmered then lit up. I was enveloped in light and I blinked, and when my eyes opened I was on the edge of a sprawling garden: a lawn greener than green, a gazebo in one corner and a set of lawn furniture right in the center. Behind it, a colonial-style mansion.

I took a breath and looked up at the blue sky.

'I hate day work,' I said.

—Job is the job, bud, said the voice in my ear.

'Yep. Just feels… wrong, know what I mean? Like, you wouldn't go to watch a football game in the middle of the night, would you?'

—Afraid your sins might be exposed to the light, is that it? He chuckled.

'Maybe.'

—Yeah well. Deep in the Structure, you're the only god. No one else here to judge you.

'No one but me.'

—Now's not the time to get philosophical. We got a job to do. Go ahead and run a few tests so we can get going.

'Sure.'

I had a good look up at the house before I moved. No matter how many times I did this, there was always the sense of eyes on me. As usual, I saw nothing. I went to the rose bush by the hedge only feet away and plucked a fresh rose. I took a sniff.

—Smell anything?

'No.'

—Good.

I held it out in front of me, twirled it once in my hand and let go. It floated softly skyward.

—Looks good from here.

'Yeah I think we're good,' I said.

—Let's check airtime then we'll get going.

'Right here? In the garden?'

—There's no one to see you, partner. At least not until you want them to.

I bent my knees and pushed off the ground, and found myself soaring into the air.

—Look at you, you sexy bald fucking eagle…

'Fuck you.' I maneuvered myself groundward and landed on two feet.

—Yeah, I'd say you're good to go.

'I hear you. Let's do this then.'

—Go for it, killer.

I took off my jacket and threw it in the bush. I don't know why when I entered the Structure I was always dressed so inappropriately. Some kind of latent narcissism, I guessed. I kept close to the line of the hedge up through the garden. I knew where they'd be waiting. We'd built the dream, after all. It was our show. Still, your mind runs away with you and you invent all kinds of shit in your head. There's no accounting for the subconscious.

I reached the house and had a look in the window. It looked into his study. I knew this because I'd studied the house. I'd studied everything. The more you know about a target, the more you can dictate the outcome of his subconscious. It's not rocket science. Well, it's a science of sorts, but it's mostly will. Pure, unrelenting violence of will. That's what wins in this game.

The study was wall-to-wall shelves. Guy had a lot of books. Judges and lawyers always did.

I heard a noise overhead and spun around. A piano about the size of a house sailed over me, from it a deafening sound like gravel falling on a hardwood floor.

'Jesus Christ,' I said, leaning against the window.

—Seeing some weird shit, partner?

'Yeah. Sometimes I wonder why I don't just get a normal job.'

—'Cause sick assholes like you don't do normal.

I sighed. 'Yeah.' I looked down at my belt. A machete materialized there.

—See what I mean, huh? You animal. Now, let's go get dirty.

'Right.'

I moved along the wall of the house to the gate and opened it quietly. Slipped through. Shuffled along the gable wall. I peered around the corner, gasping when I saw the view: the patio overlooking the ocean, beyond a volcanic island rising from the sea like Atlantis, two moons behind it, glimmering in the silver water of the ocean.

—Pretty out there, huh?

'Unbelievable.'

—Don't get too hung up on it. This guy's living in a fantasy world.

'I'd wake up to this fantasy any day. No problem.'

—Stay on task. You see the mark?

I turned my head. There they were, just as planned. The judge, sitting on the patio having breakfast, next to him his mother. I shook my head.

—How do you feel about cutting up old ladies?

I sighed. 'Beats decapitating children, don't you think?'

He chuckled. —Hey, whatever gets you off. You know, I'd say the children might almost be easier, in a way. For a man like you or me.

'Yeah? How do you figure?'

—'Cause we've all had a mother, right? You and me, we've never had kids, and we don't feel the attachment to them that parents have. A mother, on the other hand, we've both had one of those. Not so easy to cut up an old woman who reminds you of your mother.

'My mother was a bitch,' I said.

—Aww, hear the tiny fiddles play? You're such a cliché, Vangelis. You know what, why don't you let me into your dreams one day and I'll go to work on your mother for you. You can even watch.

'You're a sick fuck, DP. Maybe you should be in here instead of me.'

—Naw. I'm a technician, partner. You're the one that does the dirty work.

My hand slid down to the hilt of the machete as I watched them eat breakfast. I'd never worked on an old woman before. Had no idea how I'd feel about it.

'Much as I like chatting with you, DP, I've gotta job to do.'

—Then go fucking do it.

I raised a hand to my ear and touched the lobe. It went quiet.

I looked out over the sea toward the island and sighed. People's subconscious could be really beautiful. In the far distance I saw two figures sprint across the sky as if in a race. I smiled. Then I turned back to the pair on the patio. I heard music now, something classical that drifted from the window behind them. I composed myself and stepped out from behind the gable wall. Time to get to work.

I walked across the grass toward them. Felt like I was walking on cotton wool.

I'd almost reached the table when he turned his head from the ocean to see me. He stood up quickly, knocking over his chair. His mother didn't move.

'No no,' I said, putting my hand on the handle of the machete. 'Don't be getting up.' I pointed to the chair. 'Pick it up and sit down.'

He looked at me for a second then turned and righted the chair. He sat, not taking his eyes from me.

'Who are you?'

'I'm just passing through,' I said.

The old lady smiled at me. 'Are you a colleague of James's, dear?' She turned to her son. 'Why don't you offer our guest a cup of tea?'

I held up my hand. 'Don't worry, ma'am. I won't be stopping long.' I looked at him. I could see the fear in his eyes.

'I was stabbed in the thigh by my sister at the age of five,' he said. 'She stabbed me with scissors.'

Sometimes people said the weirdest shit in dreams. There was only one way to counter it.

'When I was four I bit a hummingbird in two pieces,' I told him. 'One part disappeared and I kept the other under my pillow and forgot about it. Turned out it was whispering shit to me for years in my sleep. I fell into psychosis and woke up in an asylum an old man.'

He shook his head. 'Do you have a lawyer?'

His mother tutted. 'Now now, James, we don't talk work at the breakfast table, you know that.'

'Yes mother.'

'You know, maybe I will have some tea.' I picked up the old lady's cup and took a sip, and placed it back on the table.

'Burdock.'

'Helps purify the blood,' the old lady said.

'Oh yeah? If you don't mind me saying, ma'am, you look like you live well. What would you need to purify your blood for?'

'We are all polluted,' she said. She opened her mouth and a daffodil grew from her throat.

'I see.' I turned to him.

'Why are you here interrupting breakfast?'

Lucent. More than normal. Best not hang about. 'Funny you should ask that,' I said.

I took a step toward his mother, took her hand and placed it on the table. With a single flourish I pulled the machete from my belt, spun it, and brought it down on her arm right above the wrist. Cleaved it right off. Blood shot from the wound. She looked up at me and smiled. I looked at the judge, who was up out of his seat, eyes frozen in horror.

Now the clock was ticking.

'Remember all that shit that went down in Rwanda years back?' I said to him as I circled his mother to the other side, putting a hand on her shoulder as I did. (I had a speech for all occasions.) 'Those men were under orders to slaughter without prejudice, and they did – a million people in a hundred days.'

I lifted his mother's other hand and placed it on the table, now swimming in the blood that ran from her severed limb. The sky became darker as I spoke.

'But not only did they kill, they went out of their way to amputate and disfigure, cutting off arms and legs with scythes and machetes, and when they had no machetes they used clubs and even rocks… I mean, can you imagine having your arm amputated with a rock? You should count yourself lucky I'm not a sadist…'

I raised the machete and brought it down on her arm right below the elbow. I looked in her eyes as I did it. She was still smiling. I turned to see him take a lunge toward me. As his foot hit the ground, he froze. The whole place shook as if an earthquake had struck deep underground. The judge inched forward in super slow motion, just like in a dream.

DP broke into the sequence. —He's close to snapping, Vangelis…

'Shut up and don't interrupt again DP. I got this.' I tapped my ear.

I looked at him. His eyes were locked on me, the shock gone, the fight-or-flight response kicking in. You can tell a man's true nature by how he responds to such a situation. If he was made of stronger stuff, his hands would already be around my throat.

I took the old woman by the hair. She was still grinning. I smiled at her then turned to him.

'We all lose what we love, James. Sometimes it's easier to just *let go*. Save yourself the pain.'

It was getting darker by the second. I lifted the blade to her throat. Her mouth was open and a song was coming out: *Over the Rainbow*. I looked at him.

'What do you say, James?'

His movements were imperceptible but it was all in his eyes. I ran the long edge of the blade across her throat. Suddenly I felt the heat of her head in my hand. My stomach tightened. In a split second the judge had his hands around my throat. We fell to the ground. With my blade raised defensively, it slipped into his eye socket. Everything went black momentarily as the earth shook. Then the blinding sideways light. I opened my eyes in the dim Subversion room at Vathos.

'You woke him, you fucking idiot,' said DP. He hopped up out of his chair and hurried over.

'It was an accident.'

'Accidents don't happen on this job. You know that.' He reached behind my neck and pulled off the epidural.

'Sometimes shit goes wonky,' I said.

'Save it for Emerson. You know he's gonna haul you in, right?'

'Yeah. I know it.'

I sat up and sighed, and touched the back of my neck.

'That was almost textbook up until you fucked it,' DP said.

I got pissed. 'Drop it. I'll take it from Emerson. I don't need it from you.'

DP held up his hands. 'You're the killer, partner.'

He sat down at his chair and swiveled to the monitors. I looked over his shoulder to see the grainy image of me with the blade at the old lady's throat. He'd be cutting it up and sending a recording to Emerson. For the records.

I shook my head. 'Fuck.' Over my shoulder: 'See you later.'

'Yep. Keep your head up, partner.'

I opened the door to the bright lights of the corridor.

2

Good thing about working nights is breakfast alone. No one's out at five in the morning, and if you've got a good deli nearby you pretty much got the place to yourself.

I leave Vathos and drive over to the little Mexican cantina next to the abandoned stadium. There are two others in there sitting at the back table. I give them a quick once over before I sit down: they're not eating, not speaking, only sitting looking out the window. I look up to catch the waitress's eye.

'Hola.'

'Hola.'

I sit down. She comes over and pours me a coffee.

'Que quieres?'

I give her my order and she takes it to the kitchen. I turn to the two men at the back of the cantina: still silent, still staring out at the cold street. Such is the malaise at five in the morning when you come off night shift. Much is contained in their silence. I too slip into that malaise and turn to look out the window. The hulking shoulder of the stadium rises up above the cantina, above it the first cobalt hue of daybreak. I look down to find I'm pinching the flesh between my thumb and forefinger. I let off, placing my two hands on the table. Fucking job. Emerson would come down on me hard for that slip. It was my first to be fair. Maybe I got slack, overconfident.

Not much to keep you on your guard when you're slicing up an old lady in front of a weak-minded judge. Maybe it was just that – carelessness. Certainly not incompetence. I sighed and looked out the window.

'Fuck it,' I whispered. Holding onto things, like I always did. But what of it? Emerson would give me shit and in a day or two it'd be forgotten. Forget the black mark on your record. After six months it'd be gone.

The waitress appeared at my shoulder and put down the eggs.

'Huevos,' she said. She put down a plate of tortillas.

'Gracias.'

My hunger wasn't what it normally was but I ripped into it all the same. If I didn't eat I wouldn't sleep. My routine was different from most. I ate breakfast before going to bed. It felt perfectly natural.

'Mas café?' she said.

'No gracias.'

The light was well up by the time I left and I drove straight home and got into bed. I dunno how long I slept, but asleep or not I was still awaiting that call, so when the phone rang at fuck-knows-what hour, I rolled over and picked it up without a pause.

'Yeah?'

'Boss wants to see you.'

'You know the policy on waking an agent after his shift, don't you?'

'Don't get smart, Vangelis. Get your ass down here.'

'And why is it you calling me, Sura?'

She hung up. I put down the phone. Breach of protocol for a simple slip-up. Felt like overkill.

Within the hour, I was pulling into the car park. It hadn't even gone nine when I was waved into Emerson's office. He was sitting behind the desk with that big cumbersome head of his, looking at his monitor. I couldn't see it, but I knew what he'd be looking at. He shook his head. So he was gonna be dramatic about it.

I remained standing, hands fidgeting behind my back. Never quite knew how to stand to take a ball-busting.

At last his finger came from between his teeth to point at the screen. He still didn't look at me.

'Wanna explain this to me?'

I took a deep breath. 'Captain, I—'

'I mean, what the fuck were you thinking? Putting a machete through his *eye*…'

'Captain, you can see he more or less *fell* on the blade. He was on me like a shot and we went down together, and it just kinda slipped in…'

'Shut it, Zervas. Don't tell me it just "slipped in". That doesn't happen on this job. You're trained, are you not?'

'Yes sir.'

'How long was your training?'

'Six months sir.'

'And do you know how much we spent on your training?'

'No sir.'

He paused here and stared at me. 'I'll tell you, Zervas, and I never told this to an operative before – 600,000 dollars. That's what it costs to get one of you assholes to the level of professionalism we need to do what we do. Yeah you heard me right, asshole – six hundred grand. On your physical training, neurobiological awareness, cerebral alteration, electrical synthesis, encephalographic analysis, REM manipulation training – you remember all that, don't you? You should, because some of it is very fucking painful. And you went through it all because the scientists – not me – deemed you most worthy, out of 327 applicants – most of whom, I might add, came from military and intelligence backgrounds – to come and work here at Vathos as an infiltration asset. And in order to do that, they threw obscene – I mean *obscene* – amounts of money at you—'

'Sir…'

'Don't you fucking dare interrupt me.'

'Yes sir.'

'...And the idea behind this ridiculous investment is that by doing so they eliminate any and all propensity for fuck-ups. So tell me, agent, how the fuck is it that after this money was showered on you – which is more than my annual salary, by the way – how is it that you can make a monumental shitshow like this?'

'May I speak sir?'

He leaned back in his chair. 'Are you being funny?'

'No sir.'

A long foul stare. 'I asked you a direct question, agent, so yes, you may fucking speak.'

I cleared my throat. 'Sir, training teaches us that while an operative may alleviate between 96 and 97 percent of variables in an operation, the possibility always remains that a target may utilize that three of four percent uncertainly to manipulate the course or outcome of a dream to their advantage.'

'Is that so, Zervas, is that so? Just give me a minute, will you?'

He pushed a button on the intercom on his desk. 'Alina?'

'Sir?' came the voice.

'You have Agent Keane at hand?'

'Sir, I'll find her for you right now.'

'Do.'

It was eighty-three seconds between the time that the captain let off the intercom and Agent Keane arrived. We sat in silence and he stared at me. I felt every torturous second of it.

The relief when I heard the knock on the door.

'Come in.'

Sura came in and stood beside me and nodded. 'Sir.'

'Agent Keane. Let me ask you a question. Zervas here is throwing statistics at me, so since he likes to talk numbers, let me ask you a question: What's the probability of your operational success, in this case, if Subversion operations are completed without a hitch?'

Sura nodded once. I looked at the wall straight ahead as she spoke.

'Sir, in this case and with these particular variables, about 83 percent.'

'And if Zervas here fucks up like he has – and you've seen the footage, Agent Keane – what is your probability then?'

'Probability of success has dropped to 71 percent, sir.'

He turned to me. 'You hear that, Zervas? You like those numbers, huh? And do you know what that means?'

'Yes sir.'

'It means that Agent Keane here and her team have to clean up the bag of shit you've left on their doorstep. Doesn't it?'

'Yes sir.'

'Do *you* like cleaning up other people's shit, Zervas?'

'No sir.'

'Nobody does, you fucking incompetent.'

I bit my lip.

'Now, you're gonna go with Agent Keane here and she's gonna brief you on whatever it is you need to do to make this right. And believe me, whatever it is, you best get doing it. If she says you gotta go three straight hours in the chair, then you do it. That's her call. You hear me?'

'Yes sir.'

'And Zervas, I'm putting you in for a reappraisal—'

'Sir—'

'Shut it, Zervas. This is standard procedure. You make an error like this and they gotta stress-test you again. Protocol. You got me?'

'Yes sir.'

'Get outta here. Take him through what you need, Agent Keane.'

'Yes sir.'

'Go on and get outta here.'

'Sir.'

We turned. I followed Keane out. When the door was shut, I caught her grin.

'Fuck you,' I said.

'Hey, don't get mad at me. You're the one who slipped up.'

'You didn't have to make it more difficult.'

'He asked me the numbers and I told him. The numbers is the numbers.'

'And why was it you calling me this morning?'

'I'm a agent like you. I take orders just the same.'

I flexed my neck. 'Fine. So, what is it you'd have me do?'

'I don't like it.'

'Well that's tough shit, isn't it?' Sura raised a single eyebrow.

'It's a breach of protocol, Sura.'

'Emerson's already signed off on it.'

'What do Analytics have to say?'

She held up a hand. 'It was Analytics suggested it. They ran the numbers. The numbers said it would restore balance to the op.'

'To *your* op. It'll work against me next time I go in.'

'It was your fuck-up, Vangelis. And besides, we're all working on the same op.'

'Shit.' I shook my head.

'Come on.'

She took me upstairs. Analeptics – what we casually referred to as 'ground-floor' – was quiet during the day. Agents were all out on the job, and there were only a few analysts floating around. Sura took me to an empty operations room and sat me down.

'Wait here til I get the files.'

'Sure. Not going anywhere,' I said.

She left, and I got up to take a look at the boards on the wall. Depending on the operation, this too might have been a breach of protocol – an agent from Subversion given access to the inner workings of Analeptics. It was probably an expired

14

job, and if I wasn't pissed off at management right then, I'd have sat down and left it well alone. Much of it was numbers and above my head. Despite me shouting my mouth off in Emerson's office, I wasn't a numbers guy and was aware of only that which was essential for my training and operational procedure. I looked at the photos. Above them the name of the operation: *Sandman 13*. Didn't have a great deal of imagination these people. Target: Vincent deFri—

'Maybe you should leave that stuff alone.'

Sura was in the doorway. I turned. Behind her was another woman.

'Maybe you shouldn't turn me loose in Analeptics unsupervised.'

Sura came in, the other following behind her.

'You're in enough shit with Emerson, Agent Zervas. Maybe don't push your luck.'

'We reverting to surnames, are we?'

'This is Natalie Carter, Agent Zervas. She's attorney for the defense.'

'In the…?'

'Yes. She's also one of us.'

'Ah.'

I didn't know much about the workings of Analeptics, but I knew much of it was infiltration. For a job like this, they'd probably been grooming Natalie for years.

Natalie held out her hand. We shook.

'Not often we get to cross paths with ground-floor on the same operation,' I said. 'This is… strange.'

She nodded. 'The circumstances call for it, I think. Don't you?'

I repressed a sneer, and merely grinned. 'Is everyone around here aware of what happened last night?'

'We have to be,' Sura said. 'The whole operation must be readjusted.'

'Touché.'

'Don't be touchy, Zervas. We're all professionals here.'

'Oh yes we are.'

'Let's sit down, shall we?'

Sura sat and Natalie followed. I fought the urge to remain standing, and sat too. *Tail between your legs, dipshit. Just do what you're told.*

Sura laid a folder on the table and opened it. 'So, as I said, Natalie's attorney for the defense…'

'What's the case?'

'You don't need to know, Zervas. That said, with the information I'm about to give you, you can certainly find out. But in order to preserve integrity between the departments, I'm suggesting you don't go digging. You know the reason why. So…'

I glanced at Natalie. She sat very much like a lawyer. I don't know why I'd never noticed it before, but now it occurred to me they all sat the same. Natalie looked at me. Very contained in her composure. I'm sure she knew her way around a courtroom.

Sura slipped a piece of paper from the folder.

'This is a floor plan of the courthouse. Familiarize yourself with it. You'll need to look like you belong there.'

'I'm gonna be in court?'

'You're gonna make a surprise appearance, yes. This Friday.'

'That's the day after tomorrow.'

'Yes. We need it to be soon, while the dream is still fresh in the target's mind. You know, the one where you cut off his mother's arms?'

'You shouldn't be privy to the ins and outs of what we do.'

She gave me a taut grin. 'Again, circumstances.' She pushed the piece of paper toward me. 'Like I said, familiarize yourself with it, learn it inside out. Natalie's arranged to take you down there tomorrow to give you a tour, walk you around a little, get you familiar with the room.'

'Okay. So what am I doing?'

'Just this, and only this: Midway proceedings on Friday

you're gonna walk into the courtroom, hurry up the aisle to the attorney for the defense…' She gestured to Natalie. '…You're gonna press a piece of paper into her hand, and before you turn to go, you're gonna make eye contact with the judge for no less than – and this is important – *two seconds*, and then you're gonna turn and leave.'

'I'm gonna trigger him.'

'Yes. He's gonna see you, and whether he remembers his dream or not we have no way of knowing, but according to Analytics we have an 87 percent chance of restoring the operational balance by this simple intervention.'

'That's pretty cunning,' I said. 'What if he somehow recognizes me and orders that I be detained?'

'He won't. Who sees someone they thought they saw in a dream and waylays them in real life?' Sura said.

I shook my head. I knew it was a game of chance. 'Go on. Give me the numbers.'

'Analytics say that there's less than a six percent chance he'll intervene.'

I blew air out through my teeth. 'Still a greater chance than there was of things going wrong for me in the Structure last night.'

Sura turned tense. 'Maybe it's not the numbers but this negativity you're displaying that's seeping into your work and sabotaging operations, Zervas. Forget the numbers. Can you do the job or not?'

My reply was terse. 'I'll do it.'

She nodded and turned back to Natalie. 'Obviously Natalie is gonna be expecting you, but she'll act surprised to see you on the day. Now it probably goes without saying, the message you hand her is not the point of the intervention, but Zervas, don't be handing her a blank piece of paper. It'll only take one guard to look over her shoulder and see it to suspect something is going on. And a single look from the guard to the judge could sabotage the whole operation. So make it look real.'

'You're right. It does go without saying, Keane.'

She closed the folder. 'Any more questions?'

I shook my head. 'Nah. I got it.'

'Good. I've given Natalie your number. She'll meet you at the courthouse tomorrow at eleven. Just a walk, that's all. You back in tonight?'

I shook my head. 'Analytics are recalibrating. We go back in tomorrow.'

'You gonna be fresh for the courthouse appearance on Friday?'

'Yeah. I'll be alright.'

'Good then.'

We all stood up. I reached across the table to shake Natalie's hand. 'Pleasure to meet you. See you tomorrow.'

'I guess you'll be getting back to bed.' Sura looked at me and raised an eyebrow.

'Yes boss.'

'Asshole,' she muttered when Natalie had stepped away.

I turned toward the door.

'Always a pleasure working with ground-floor,' I said.

3

Natalie passed with a coffee in her hand. Saw me too, but hardly even registered my being there. Highly professional. I'd no idea what Vathos had thrown at her in training, but it was money well spent. I knew she wouldn't give anything away when I reached over her shoulder with that note.

The day was dry and the sky clear. I was sitting across the street from the courthouse, an untouched coffee on the table in front of me. Dressed in a navy-blue suit. I hated blue suits and the men who wore them. There was something sinister about them. It marked the wearer with a certain stigma; what a blue suit said was, 'I'm moving up in the world and I'll walk all over you to get where I'm going'. Especially if the blue suit is paired with brown wingtips. I was confused as to why Analytics had me in blue, but hey, I was just a grunt and didn't ask questions. *You want navy blue, I'll put on navy blue.*

Waiting. Natalie would send a text message when proceedings had been underway for exactly fifty minutes. I took the piece of blank paper from my pocket and placed it on the table, and took out a pen. I glanced across at the courthouse before putting pen to paper:

Our friend is in deep. Needs help.

Shall we meet at 6? You're my guardian angel.

Too cryptic? Nah. It would do. She wouldn't even read it.

No one would. And if they did, it would tell them nothing. I slipped the pen back in my breast pocket, folded the paper twice and put it away. Now I needed only await the text message.

When the message came I got up, checked my pocket, and set out across the street. People had been coming and going all morning through the courthouse doors. I went up the steps, taking the security pass from my pocket and draping it over my neck. I went straight in the door and up the stairs.

The building was spacious and airy. Austere. The roof a glass dome, the floors mock marble. Performative, mostly. Makes you feel like you're in a movie. And on one level, you are.

Courtroom number 3. The security guy gives my pass a cursory glance. Nods. Steps aside and I open the door. I step in, close the door carefully behind me. Maintain the decorum. Show the appropriate reverence for the proceedings.

I march discreetly up the central aisle. Make fleeting eye contact with the judge when he looks my way. Don't engage just yet. But I caught the flinch when he saw me walk toward him. I'm not looking at him now, I'm looking at the back of Natalie's head. His eyes are on me. I feel his instinctual revulsion. The attorney for the prosecution is interrogating a witness. He pays me no heed. I nod to the security guy by the gate, hold up my pass, he nods back and I pass through. The judge's eyes still on me. I take the note from my pocket, come up behind Natalie and lean over her shoulder. Place the note on the desk. I whisper an inanity in her ear: *I have a message. I await your reply.* My head is so close to her hair that no one may read my lips. The raspberry smell of her hair.

My message delivered, I look up and catch his eye. I hold it. His eyes narrow. Fear there. Somewhere, a deep recognition, a buried horror. *One second.* He's grasping desperately, trying to place my face. It has triggered him but he can't recollect the subconscious information. Suspicion, fear, anger and loathing, terror… It's all there, writhing like a poisonous and tumorous serpent inside his mind. His eyes darken and narrow further, then they open wide. *Two seconds.*

I break eye contact, turn and walk back through the gate.

The attorney still cross-examining the witness. Eyes boring into my back. Tense now. The not knowing. I can feel the weight of his fear and horror threatening to bear down on me. My steps heavier. My palms go damp. My gait with the tiniest hesitancy.

And then my hand on the door handle.

I step out.

Outside, I close the door behind me and take a deep and frantic breath.

DP phoned. Told me not to come in. There was no operation planned for that night, but depending on outcomes we might have been called up. Analytics ran the numbers and made the call to leave it alone and go back in Monday. That's all we got. No reasoning, no whys, just the order.

'You got the weekend off, partner. Go and let the hair down,' he said.

'I might just do that, DP. See you.'

I hung up and went and lay on the bed. A three-day hole to fill. I took a deep breath, closed my eyes and began my breathing. Sometimes sleep doesn't come easy to one who works in dreams. Especially if your routine is broken. But mostly because shit comes back to haunt you when you close your eyes. Shit you're better off forgetting. As it is, the mind is not prone to such cooperation. Even rooting around in the filth and detritus of the mind like I do nightly, I've still little idea of the deep mechanics of it all. It all happens below. Below the monotonous habitual workings of the conscious mind, the subconscious is whirring – one million new synaptic connections made every second: viewing, assessing, connecting, assimilating, processing, calculating… it's a machine we've almost zero understanding of. And the more you learn of it, the more frightening it becomes. Which is why, when a man like me comes home from doing what he does most nights, it becomes difficult to close one's eyes. Doors are open in my own mind that aren't in other people's. Doors that descend to deep inaccessible places that are better left unexplored. It takes a brave man to venture into someone else's dreams. It takes a braver man to delve into his own.

By monitoring my breathing I nodded off and slept for several hours. After, I got up and made something to eat. By the time I was done it was almost dark, and I sat down and watched the sky outside turn purple then dark blue then black. Nighttime was a good time to go out. A man like me is comfortable in the dark. Day holds a certain unreality when you spend nights in the dreamtime of someone else's head. Day can be painful. Night does not hold the same uncertainties.

I phoned ahead, told Roche I was coming. Roche'd usually make time for me after dark. I was her magnus opus, after all. Her ongoing masterpiece. Her work-in-progress that would never be finished.

Roche's place was out back of The Nationale, a Michelin-starred French restaurant in the old quarter. Down the back alley where the bins for the restaurant sat in a row, Roche's place was discreet and nondescript: no signage, no opening times; the only indication of what lay within was a tattered decal of a needle on the reinforced glass window. I tried the door then knocked, and Roche appeared from the back room. I looked at her through the window. She didn't make eye contact. She looked in a foul mood too which meant I was in for a rough couple of hours. She opened the door wordlessly and gestured inside.

'Roche,' I said in greeting.

I stepped in, took off my jacket and hung it. She locked the door and led me wordlessly through the tatty reception into the back room. Not a place would be your go-to choice for your first tattoo. But all those who knew her rep came to Roche Ma. She did all the Triad guys in the city. Sleeves, shoulders, thighs – she did it all. I'd commissioned her with a backpiece a few years before with the simple instructions: I want you to make something grotesque. She went to work. Every week, or every month, whenever I had time, I'd come down and we'd do another couple of inches. Two years in we still weren't finished. And to be honest, I was kinda tired of the whole thing, but I'd started so I'd goddamned well finish it. We were about three-quarters done.

Roche sat and lit a cigarette and prepped her needles. I took off my tee and lay on the table. She turned and moved the dentist's lamp over my torso and ran her hand over my back.

'How's it lookin'?'

She sighed. 'Ugly.' A woman of few words.

'That's what I asked for.'

Truth, I'd never seen it. Swore I wouldn't look at it til it was finished. And I hadn't. Times I was tempted when I stepped out of the shower, but I always resisted. Soon it was forgotten. The only time it came to mind was for a day or two after the work when the inflammation was bad and it was all swollen up. Once that passed, I forgot it.

Roche tested the gun. I listened to the vile buzz and felt it in my scrotum. Muscle memory. The machine hissed a few more times then she put it down. She ran a disposable razor over a small area of my back just below the right shoulder blade then wiped it down. Her hands traced the length of my back as she appraised the work in its totality and considered how she'd proceed. So far as I knew, she was winging it.

'Aren't you curious?' she said.

'Only when you're working. Once I step outside, I forget all about it.'

'Hmm.'

She picked up the cigarette, took a last draw, and stubbed it out. She lowered the hood of her hoodie and tied back her hair, put on a pair of black latex gloves. She picked up the gun, tested it a few times, then rested her elbows on my back. Then she went to work. I gritted my teeth and settled in for the next two hours.

Roche rubbed the area down with cream and bandaged it up. She finished same as she always did:

'Someday it will be finished. But not today,' she said.

Somehow it always sounded enigmatic.

'We're in no rush for that day to come,' I said.

'You are strange.'

'And you are a mystery to me, Roche.'

'Wanna smoke a joint?'

'You know I don't like that stuff.'

She waved a hand. 'It's very smooth, very easy stuff. You will like it.'

'Why not then,' I said.

She took the machine apart and put the needles in the sterilizer, and wiped down the table and her working surface, and when her tools were packed away she took off her gloves and put everything in the bin. I put on my T-shirt and sat there in silence as she took out her weed and began to roll.

'Don't you want to know what I'm painting on you?' she said as she busied herself.

'No.'

'Why? Are you only here for the pain?'

'I'm not interested in pain.'

'Self-punishment? What?'

Two years to get to this conversation. 'I want a record of horror on my body,' I said. 'I want there to be on my body a testimony of the worst things that man is capable of.'

She looked up at me. 'So that your soul will seem clean in comparison?'

I smiled. Her narrow eyes saw much. She licked the rolling paper and with a flick of the hand created a tight little spliff. She twisted off the top and inserted a roach, then turned and rolled on her chair toward the couch on which I sat. Pulling out a lighter, she lit the joint and took a long hit on it. Then she passed it to me.

'You read Dante?' she asked.

I shook my head. 'That what you're painting on my back? The seven circles of hell?'

She was still blowing smoke through her nose. 'You asked me not to tell you and so I don't tell you,' she said. 'But you should read Dante.'

I took a hit of the joint and passed it back. Sickly sweet and heavy. It was something I liked the smell of but had never really taken to as a recreation.

'I don't do much reading.'

'You should read.'

'I'm not sure I've got the stomach for epic poetry.'

'I can tell you have a strong stomach,' she said, and nodded slowly as she looked me in the eye.

'Oh yeah?'

She turned to the bookshelf that sat above her worktop and gazed along its length. If she was looking for Dante, she didn't find it. She turned to me and handed back the joint. I took it, sucked on it, gave it back.

'Enough for me,' I said. 'You kill it.'

'I will kill it,' she said. She regarded me through the haze. 'What do you do for fun?'

This was the most we'd ever spoken.

I shook my head. 'I come here, Roche. I come here and let you turn my body into a work of art.'

'I mean when you're not punishing yourself.'

'This isn't punishment, I told you.'

'You said. What I'm getting at is, who do you like to fuck?'

'I don't do much fucking, truth be told, Roche. My job kinda kills my social life, know what I mean?'

She shrugged. 'Wanna fuck?'

We fucked. We fucked, and after we lay on her bed in the room above her studio, me on my belly and her naked against my side. She looked over my back, ran her hands over it and scratched it with her nails. We lay silently in the spent aftermath of sex as she regarded her handiwork. I said nothing. It was nice just to be touched. I fell asleep for a bit and when I woke she was still lying on her side. She dug her nails into the flesh of my shoulder.

'Are you planning the next part of the tattoo?' I said.

'I don't plan.'

'Why do you keep looking at it?'

'Because it's my story. And I don't know what's going to happen.'

'The story is telling itself?'

'Yes.'

'And you do not dictate the ending.'

'No.'

'Are you curious what will happen?'

'Yes.'

I nodded. 'You're an artist.'

'I'm a storyteller.' She rolled onto her back, picked up a cigarette and lit it. I turned onto my side and took her tiny tit in my hand and squeezed her nipple. Her body was clean as fresh snow, save for a tiny fish on the inside of her right wrist.

'Why don't you have more tattoos?' I said.

She shook her head. 'They bore me. I only like telling stories.'

'Tell me a story,' I said.

'You already have your story. And it is the worst I ever told.'

4

I walked into the office with DP. Seated at a table were Maynes, head of Subversion, and Gottfried, Analytics. Standard operational planning. DP closed the door behind us.

'Sit down,' Maynes said.

I nodded. 'Boss.'

We sat.

'So, I've been informed about your intervention with Analeptics and that it all went according to plan,' Maynes said. 'Now, that's all hunky-dory, but it doesn't rule out that things may have changed significantly on our side, but Analytics have looked into it and they're convinced it'll not tip the scales too much either way.' He turned to Gottfried. 'You wanna say a little more about that?'

Gottfried nodded. 'Marks don't usually encounter our agents in everyday life, but since we often dream about people we encounter day to day, this shouldn't be too alarming to the target. The only difference in this case, is that he first dreamed about you then encountered you in waking life. Now, our ability to deceive ourselves is so great that the target has probably already put you out of mind and forgotten about you, at least on a conscious level. He won't have allowed himself to believe he could have dreamed someone then watched while that person walked into his courtroom. It's simply ridiculous.

That said, his subconscious mind will be aware that this is exactly what happened, and it's the subconscious of course that we're most concerned with in Subversion operations.'

Gottfried paused to push his glasses up his nose. He opened the file in front of him.

'And that is why,' he continued, 'we're gonna have you dressed for the follow-up operation exactly as you were dressed when you walked into the courtroom, right down to the pen that was in your breast pocket...'

'How did you know about that?' I said.

'We know everything, Zervas. Because we have to,' Maynes said.

'The subconscious mind is composed, among other things,' said Gottfried, 'of millions of cognitive recollections, and in nanoseconds can compile, analyze, and cross-reference thousands of experiential events for situational awareness and threat analysis. The fewer new synaptic connections the brain is forced to create, the less chance we have of upsetting operational success. So let's not change anything. Let's keep things as simple as we can. We've had enough variables in this operation already.'

I raised an eyebrow. Sounded like a dig at me.

Maynes pushed two folders across the table and opened the one in front of him. DP and I followed suit.

Maynes spoke. 'We've identified an avenue we think worth pursuing. Well, it was clear all along, but we just didn't have the angle from which to attack it.'

Gottfried took over. 'Following a search of the hard-copy medical records in the vaults at city hall, we discovered a file on the target from early childhood. It seemed he was admitted to St Charles' Hospital fifty-one years ago after an accident at a playground.'

Maynes: 'Our judge was climbing over the fence of said playground when he slipped and impaled himself on the railing somewhere between his anus and his testicles. He was eight years old. We figure this is the underlying reason he never married. Aside from the reduction in his virility, we think the accident produced a trauma that affected his sex life right into adulthood.'

Maynes paused, took a sip of water. He tilted his head in a strange manner, as if humored by the theory.

Gottfried: 'We contend that if we recreate this accident in a torture scenario, we can produce the manipulative potential that Analeptics require for operational success. That is our next scenario.'

I flicked through the folder for the details. Specifically, what age the judge would be in the dream sequence. I found it.

'Fifteen,' I said. 'You want me to sexually torture a fifteen-year-old. In my blue cashmere suit.'

'Problem, Zervas?'

'No.' I shook my head. 'Not really. I am somewhat concerned about the suit, I should say. That was an expensive investment, and if I'm gonna be making a mess of it when I'm under, then I'm gonna have to insist—'

Seeing the look on Maynes' face, I shut it. Next to me, DP suppressed a chuckle.

'Now's not the time for humor, Zervas. It's your sloppiness that led to the whole operation being redrawn. So please act like you give a damn about your job.'

'Yes sir.'

I endured Maynes' glare. Maynes was ex-military. A hard case. He'd come through agent work, what I was doing now, and worked his way up to management. We'd all heard tales about shit he'd done on the job, shit you wouldn't wish on your mortal enemy. But that was in the war against the cartels – no holds barred, and with guys like that, you need to engage in some head-melting depravity to really break them. Maynes was one of those guys who could not, and never would, turn his back on the things he'd done and the things he'd seen. It was a mystery to me how he was still in management at all.

Maynes turned to Gottfried.

'So, what we propose is pretty standard. We leave the particularities of the job up to you. What we insist on is that warm-up is done with a boxcutter – we identified another instance in his childhood when he sliced his finger with a boxcutter, so it should be the ideal tool for the task – but for the finale you've got to impale him using this…'

Gottfried reached under the desk. He lifted the crown of an anti-climb fencing spike and placed it on the table. Thing looked like a steel arrow with five barbed spikes on it.

'Jesus Christ,' I said. 'You want me to shove that up his hole?'

DP winced.

'That's the job, Zervas. You do what you gotta do.'

'Yes sir.'

'Any questions?'

'Yeah…' DP pointed at the notes in the folder. '…Says here it's gonna happen in an "antique brass bed" with a portrait of Lincoln on the wall opposite. What's that about?'

'It's his grandparent's bed,' Maynes said. 'Can you do it or do you need the whole backstory too?'

DP shrugged. 'Hey, no problem here. Weird and creepy is what we do.'

Maynes closed the folder. 'Good. Then go get prepped.'

DP was a beast on the console. He mocked up the template and we ran through it together several times to nitpick on the particulars of the scene according to the operational outline provided by Analytics. 'Ambience', we liked to call it, and sometimes we took artistic license. Today we didn't. We followed Analytics' outlay to the letter. Trials were done in VR. It wasn't anything as immersive as the real thing, but it gave us a good preview of the dream scene.

Strapped into the VR, I lay down on the antique brass bed to get a view from the target's perspective.

'This is fucked up,' I said.

DP whistled. 'Sure is. I wouldn't wanna be ass-raped with

a fence spike in front of Abe Lincoln. That shit's enough to scar you for life.'

'Still, we do what we gotta do, right?'

'Right. Rather you than me. Enough that I have to watch it from a distance. You gotta look in his eyes as you do it.'

'Don't remind me.'

'Still. It's only a dream,' DP said laughing, and I joined in and we sang it together: 'It's only a *dream*…'

'And if you get lost, bud, you just click your heels together and say it three times…' DP put on his Dorothy voice: 'There's no place like home, there's no place like home…'

'Your shit is old, DP.'

'Fuck you. This is what keeps you sane, partner. If it wasn't for me, you'd have lost your shit in there a long time ago.'

'Sure DP.'

'Fuck your good self and get in the chair. I've got an alert coming through here.'

'From ground-floor?'

'Yeah.'

'What time is it?'

'Just gone ten.'

'This guy turns in early, huh?'

'Yes he does. Ground-floor are standing by.'

'Right,' I said.

I took off my shoes and sat in the chair. An alert meant Analeptics were waiting to apply the epidural. One of Sura's team would be on-site, right in his house, standing by. As soon as the target was asleep, an epidural patch would be applied to the back of his neck and this would allow us to tap into his subconscious via the cerebral cortex. The patch was biodegradable and began to dissolve upon contact with the skin. After two hours, it would completely disappear. That was more than enough time for us to get into the mark's dreams and stir shit up. Go to work. Break him down. There was no Subversion without Analeptics to do the groundwork and the follow-up, and there was no job at all without Subversion, and neither of us could do anything without Analytics. We were the golden triangle of corporate–political subterfuge.

'Ground-floor are going in.'

'Alright,' I said. I lay back. DP got up and inserted the epidural and gave me the shot, some kind of cocktail of benzodiazepines. The shot did two things: one, it made sure my pain receptors were dulled, and two, it increased synaptic adaptability in the cortex, enhancing my perception and responsiveness when under.

DP sat back down. 'Right, let's get you under…'

I shifted in the chair to get comfortable.

'Wanna play around while we wait for shit to kick in?'

'Sure,' I said. 'But nothing too fucking weird, you hear me?'

DP laughed. He'd a sick sense of humor.

'I'm serious DP. I'm not in the mood for anything crazy.'

'Hey man, it's the Structure decides, not me. I'm just the facilitator.'

'Bullshit.'

He laughed. The 'Structure' was what we called the metaconscious framework into which we were implanted before we were inserted into the target dreamscape. Metaconsciousness was a slippery and unpredictable place, and while you could mostly manipulate events inside the framework, to some extent you were at the mercy of forces beyond human control. It was an unpredictable place, and protocol decreed we were not to spend more time there than absolutely necessary. Sometimes we played around. It was a fascinating place to explore, sometimes mind-blowing.

'I'm patching you in…'

I felt a tingling sensation on the back of my neck which crept down my spine and up inside my head, and then a sudden rush…

I took a sharp intake of air in my lungs, and then…

Darkness. I would say I opened my eyes, but it wasn't exactly like that. In an instant I was bodiless. All around me was an unending black. After a few moments, a sense of the corporeal returned to me. Human consciousness is intimately tied up with bodily experience. Even in an entirely mental landscape we impose our corporeal structures. Slowly the sense of my anatomy returned. Even though they weren't there, my mind provided a torso and a heart within it, arms and legs, a head, nose eyes and ears, they all materialized. Then I felt ground underfoot.

—I'm applying residual, DP said.

'No DP—' I began, but before I could finish, the darkness softened, and I closed my eyes for a moment and opened them onto a great desert.

'Prick,' I said.

—Don't know why you're so afraid of your own headspace.

Residual was the state that contained the strongest elements of one's own subconsciousness. All the stuff that lay buried deep, deep below, that was residual. Stuff you sometimes didn't need to see.

—Jesus man. It's just one big empty down there, huh?

'Couldn't just run an old rec playthrough, huh?'

—Fuck that, man. Shit is boring. This is much more interesting.

I was standing on a rock in the middle of a vast, still and silent landscape. Out in front of me I could see the curvature of the earth. I turned. Behind me, the hint of a mountain range in the far distance, between me and the mountains, a salt lake. I looked at the sky. It reflected the silver tinge of the salt.

'I gonna die of fucking boredom in here, DP,' I said. 'Pull me out.'

—Wait a minute now, DP said. —I've just had a marvelous idea. What if we lace residual with an overlay of your last forty-eight hours, huh? That might be interesting…

'DP, I swear, if you pull up my recent memories I'll come up there and pull out your throat.'

—Jesus, man. Settle down, I was just kidding. Wait… I'm gonna have to patch you into operational. REM's reaching optimal.

'Do it.'

I felt the ground underfoot tremble very gently, right before the blinding shower hit me. I opened my eyes and I was in a house. A house dark and old.

'Grandpa's?'

—Yep. Nice suit.

I looked down at myself. 'Fuck you.'

He laughed. —How's the house lookin'?

'Much like we built it, DP.'

I was sitting in the living room in a Victorian rose-pink high-back sofa. I ran my hands over the fabric.

'I ever tell you you're something of an artist, DP?'

—No you haven't, and shame on you. All this time I thought my work was going unappreciated.

'Yeah. This is some of your best work yet.'

The house was exquisitely done: linoleum parquet, inlaid open fireplaces with tiled floor and with wall-built bookcases either side. Sash windows, sconce wall lights, picture railing and pierced moldings... no detail had been left out.

—When you're done admiring my handiwork, there's a vase of flowers on the coffee table in front of you. Check it out please.

I stood up, leaned in and took a sniff. 'Nothing,' I said.

—Good. Then let's get to work.

I went out into the hallway. Wall lights lit the stairs rising up to the first floor. I stepped onto the stairs then stopped, turning to look into a sitting room to my right.

'Who the fuck's that?' I said.

—Looks like grandma.

'What's she doing here?'

—It's just the target reacting to our intrusion. Setting up a safety net. Nothing to get alarmed about, DP said.

'Just took me unawares is all. Do you suppose the old man's about here too?'

—Could be, DP said.

'Hope you made sure he doesn't have a shotgun.'

—We've a seclusion zone set up as standard. No arms coming in or out. Only what you're carrying.

My hand went to my inside pocket, finding the boxcutter. In the other pocket, the fencing spike.

'Jesus Christ,' I said, putting a hand on it. 'This thing is gonna make shit of the lining of my suit.'

—Put a claim in, DP said, chuckling.

I got to the top of the stairs and stopped.

—Second door on your right.

'Gotcha.'

I went to the door, but stopped when I heard a noise outside the window. I went to it and looked out.

'You seeing this?' I said.

—I see it.

'A parade, in the middle of the night. In a suburban street,' I said.

—Yeah. Pay it no mind.

There was a high-school marching band on the street in the darkness. They played their instruments yet there was no music. Even the cymbals smashed together yet made no sound.

'This is a weird fucking guy.'

—Aren't we all.

I went back to the door and put my hand on the brass knob. Turned it slowly and opened, and peered inside. The boy lay there in the bed sleeping, covers pulled up around his neck. I looked around the room. Just as we'd built it. I stepped in and closed the door. There he was, old Abe on the back wall. I tipped an imaginary cap, then turned and stood at the foot of the bed.

—Time to get freaky.

I took a deep breath as I watched the boy sleep. Then a kind of shadow, momentary and fleeting, so slight I almost didn't notice it, passed the right side of the bed.

'You see that?' I said to DP.

—Nah, what is it?

'Some kind of movement by the side of the bed. Could have been a woman. You think the mark sensed ground-floor at work?'

—I doubt it. Could have been anything.

'Did you haunt this house, you prick?' I said.

I could hear him smiling when he spoke. —They'd fire my ass for that shit, partner. And anyway, I'm not that twisted.

'And yet you work for Vathos. Lying asshole.'

—Let's just do this, he said. —All the indicators are reading right, levels are optimal. Get to work, you sick fuck. Show me what you're capable of.

I went to the bedside table and laid out the boxcutter and the fence spike, then took off my jacket and laid it on the chair.

—Oh, he means business…

I opened the wardrobe behind me, took out a bedsheet and began to slice it up.

'Couldn't have just given us some rope, huh…'

—Hey, what Analytics says goes, DP said.

I cut up five lengths of sheet, and when it was ready, I tied the kid's left arm to the iron bed frame. Then his right, then his two feet.

—Good job. Now wake him.

I rolled up my sleeves. Taking the last length of sheeting, I placed it into his mouth. He opened his eyes as I slid it around his head to tie it at the front over his mouth. His eyes opened wide in terror and he began to grunt.

'Remember me?' I said. I stroked his face. He shook his head frantically and began to struggle. 'You're tied up good. You're not going anywhere.'

I straightened up, lifting the boxcutters and playing with the blade, opening and closing it. His head turned, he watched, the whites of his eyes bright in the dark room. His pupils were dilated to an insane degree. I sat on the edge of the bed and put a hand on his chest. Felt his heart racing.

'Feel that? That's nothing but your fear response taking over. Your increased heart rate is helping to pump blood around your body and glucose production has increased to ensure your body has the requisite energy for fight or flight. And do you know why? Because your amygdala has kicked in and is now making all your decisions for you. *Fear memory*. That's what we're talking about here...'

I lowered the boxcutters to his face and placed pressure on his skin just below the eye. He whimpered desperately. I pushed, not so it broke the skin but merely caused him to tense up. The muscles on his neck protruded from under the skin.

'See?' I tapped his forehead with my other hand. 'It's all in here. Every fear we've ever experienced, every trauma, all up here. Even ones we haven't experienced – DNA-based fears. Ancestral. It's amazing, you should read about it...'

I ran the blade over his face, tucking it under the gag at the corner of his mouth, and pulled lightly. His eyes scrunched closed.

'Don't look away,' I said. 'Closing your eyes won't make it go away.'

He opened his eyes narrowly and closed them again. I took the blade from his mouth. Rolling back the covers, I lifted his pajama top up to his neck to expose his torso, then placed the blade in the middle of his chest right below the neck. I ran it over his torso until it found his belly button. I dug around inside.

'You got a girlfriend, kiddo? Nice boy like you, pretty face and slim – you ain't got a girlfriend?'

—Getting a bit homoerotic in here, DP said in my ear. I ignored him.

'What's the problem? Is there something wrong with you?'

I ran the blade down over his abdomen until it was pushing down his pajama bottoms. He kicked and struggled wildly. I sighed and let off him, and sat looking at him for a bit. I could see the goosebumps that covered his torso. His skin prickled with fear and his nipples were erect. I pulled on one.

—Nice touch, DP said.

I raised the blade to his stiff nipple and made like I was about to hack it off.

'Do you know that in ancient Ireland, sucking a king's nipple was a gesture of submission to authority?' I pinched his nipple between thumb and forefinger. 'True. They found this corpse in a peat bog a few years back, the thing was 2000 years old. It was sliced in half and had been disemboweled. They could tell by his diet and his state of health that he was wealthy – I mean, kingly wealthy. But the thing is, his nipples had been sliced off too. They figure he'd given some offense, maybe to his father, maybe to the gods, so in order to make him unfit for kingship, they sliced off his nipples. Then they sacrificed him.'

I applied pressure with the blade until I saw a speck of blood form on the skin.

—Careful, DP said. —Remember what happened last time.

I let off and stood up. 'I think he's pissed himself,' I said. I threw the cover off the bed and pulled down his pants. The sheets were soaking.

—Didn't take much, huh? DP said.

I shook my head. The kid's penis and testicles were all shriveled up with fear. I turned away from the bed.

'Think we can cut it here, DP?' I whispered. 'He's a fucking mess.'

—Best see it through, partner. That way nothing can come back on us. Step by step, just like the book says.

I turned around. I stepped forward and rested the blade on his knee then ran it up the inside of his thigh.

'Kid like you, doesn't use his junk, best thing to do would be to *slice* it off, don't you think?'

He kicked and groaned, writhing in his own water.

—That's four uses of the trigger word, DP said. We need four more.

'Just *slice* it off and rid you of the thing, huh?' I said it as I pushed the blade into the flesh of his thigh. ''Cause you ain't got no use for it, do you?'

—Five. Keep it up.

I put the blade on the table and went over to the window. Arms folded, I stared out into the street. The marching band was still there, except now they were all standing in the front garden looking up at the bedroom window. There were two war elephants, something Hannibal might have marched over the Alps with, standing in the street under the light of the gas lamps that lined the avenue. Everyone and everything was silent.

'Seeing this DP?'

—Yeah. I see it. Kid's a strange one alright.

'I never cease to marvel.'

I heard the door open behind me. DP saw it happen.

—We got a visitor, he said, his voice panicky.

I turned, seeing the old man in the doorway. Some kind of grimace was painted on his face. One hand on the door, he looked at the kid in the bed, then up at me, the twisted grin still painted on his face.

'DP?'

—I dunno, man. I'd just kill him and be done with it.

'It's not part of the plan.'

I heard DP frantic at the console. —I'm running the numbers here, partner, and they've allowed for intrusion. Do it, just do it out of sight of the kid.

'My blade's on the bed.'

—Use your fucking hands, man.

I advanced on the old man and kicked his legs out from under him, then dragged him outside the door. Two arms around his throat, I sat on his chest and strangled him. Right before the light went out in his eyes, he raised his hand. In it was a letter.

'He's trying to give me a letter, DP.'

—Don't you fucking open that. Leave it, and get back to the kid.

The old man's dead hand fell to the floor. I got up off him and went back inside, slamming the door. Shit was getting weird. I was pissed off now. I didn't like it when things got unpredictable. The kid was still on the bed. He was frozen in a weird position, his knees partially raised off the bed and his arms pulled as close to his body as was able. He was staring open-eyed at the ceiling.

—He still with us?

I leaned in to see the kid's eyes dart left and right. 'I think so. Looks like his system's getting ready to shut down though.'

—Get this over with, man. The set piece, let's go…

I picked up the fence spike and turned to the kid. I used the tip of the weapon to turn his face toward me.

'Don't you be getting away from me now. Stay with me, you hear me?' I lifted the spike into his eye line. 'Seen one of these before?'

The kid began to cry. I closed my eyes and shook my head. 'Fuck's sake,' I said. 'This is perverse.'

—Just fucking do it.

'Know where this goes, kid?'

I slipped the spike between his thighs and moved it toward his anus. Felt it test his flesh.

Then it went dark.

I felt a momentary panic. 'No no,' I whispered. 'Not again.'

But when I didn't come around in Subversion, I knew something was wrong.

'DP? You there?'

No answer. I took a step back. Lifted my hand to my face. The spike was gone. I touched my body, found I was naked. Naked and in the dark. I reached forward to touch the bed but it was gone too. It was like the program had simply shut down.

'DP?' I said again.

No reply. Best guess, I was stuck in the Structure with some base program running and none of the operational overlays. I thought maybe a power-cut, but we'd so many backup generators that was impossible.

I reached to the floor to feel what was underfoot; it felt like cold dead flesh. Now I began to panic. I fought it down with steady breathing and closed my eyes and counted. No sense losing it now. I turned to look around me. No light in any direction. I tried to materialize a light, but to no avail. I wasn't in control of the build. I was about to sit down to think when I heard a noise in the distance, like a slow steady heartbeat in resting rhythm. I stood still and listened. Turned, listened again. At first I thought it was all around me, but the longer I listened the stronger it seemed from one particular direction. With no other choice, I walked toward it through the dense liquid black.

It was like walking over a vast corpse. The surface was flat and monotonous and with no end in sight. But the noise became louder, the beating more resonant, so I walked on, naked and helpless and lost.

I began to feel the noise. It was like a reverberation in my gut and in my chest, and it made the 'air' around me vibrate like sand. Then I hit a wall.

It was like the floor: fleshy and cold and giving to the touch. There was still no light, and I'd no idea if there was any point trying to follow it.

'Fuck this,' I said. I took a deep breath and exhaled. Then, almost instinctively, I punched the wall, my hand bursting right through it. I felt around. It was soft and fleshy just like the outside, so I began ripping chunks out of it, gouging a hole that I might climb through. The wall grew softer the deeper I went, and soon it was like punching through the pulpy flesh of a ripe plum. Frantic now, I climbed inside, ripping at the flesh as I struggled through. Only moments later, I pushed through a thin filmy wall and fell roughly onto a steel floor. I got up on my knees and wiped the syrupy residue from my face. I looked around.

It was closed on all sides. I turned to the opening I'd just crawled through, but it was solid steel wall. I pushed. No give. I turned back; a table had appeared in the center of the room. I stood up and walked toward it. There was a Dictaphone on the table. I stared at it, reluctant to pick it up.

'DP? You there?' I shouted.

The walls of the room flickered and for a split second I was in darkness again. I thought I heard the noise of a console.

'DP?'

Still nothing. The light came on again. I picked up the Dictaphone and looked at it. Then I hit play.

First only static. Then a voice. Garbled. A few words: … *smuggled… Servus…*

My name? The voice became clearer. It was machine-like, unhuman:

Parasitic communication engaged. Fervor. System A friendly to such. Subsumed within our structure…

The light flickered, going dark instantaneously, before shuddering into life again. I heard DP's voice, faraway yet distinct:

—Zervas?

'DP? Jesus fucking Christ, pull me outta here.'

I dropped the Dictaphone. His voice broke up before coming back clearer.

—I found you man, gimme a sec…

'Get me the fuck outta here DP…'

A sudden blinding flash and searing pain at the back of my skull, and I opened my eyes in the chair.

5

'We think it was a hack.'

'We think?' I said.

Emerson nodded. 'We're not 100 percent. We intercepted a partial broadcast. Given the graininess of the signal we can't make head nor tail of it, but it was definitely from outside. We're fairly certain it was a deliberate attempt at sabotage. Or intrusion.'

I looked around the table. We were all in there: Analytics, Security, DP and I, Jackson and Earlridge, Maynes and Coates, Sura and her team, and another two squads from Subversion and Analeptics. Emerson was at the head of the table.

'What does this mean for operational, sir?' Sura said.

Emerson shook his head. 'Absolutely nothing. We go on as normal. We've heightened security around all departments, particularly operational. We're confident this isn't gonna happen again. If you've any particular concerns, you can raise them with Agent Coates. Subversion, you guys see Maynes if you're worried. Analytics are running deep diagnostics on the event to see if we can't glean more information. And obviously, whatever we find will be used to develop new and improved training tools which you'll all be privy to. Until then, all I can advise is be alert, stay vigilant, and if you encounter anything out of the ordinary, then you let your supervising officer know about it. Immediately. Is that understood?'

'Yes sir.'

'Again. This is not of concern to you, at least not yet. Don't let it get in the way. You have a job to do, and I expect you to continue to do it.'

'Yes sir'.

Emerson sat back on his chair and looked around the room. 'Thank you all for coming in. I appreciate it's difficult to get you all together – you've all got competing schedules and it's costing some of you sleep, I know. But this is a serious matter and I thought it important to speak to you as a team. Because we are a team. Even if we work in the dark from each other and oftentimes seemingly at cross purposes, we're still a team. What we do and how we work affects every other aspect of our operation. But I think you all appreciate that.'

No one said anything. Emerson sighed.

'Go on, all of you get out of here. Zervas and Prestwick, you hang about.'

Everyone got up. I caught Sura's eye as she followed her team out the door. DP and I stayed seated, Emerson still in his chair. Two others stayed put: Deen, head of Analytics, and head of Security, Rodin.

Emerson folded his arms. The only one standing was Rodin.

'We're not gonna get into this now, gentlemen, we understand you must be a little frazzled at this point, but Rodin has a few initial questions before you get off. He's looking for a head start in getting to the bottom of this. Anything you can tell him, anything at all, might lead us to some real answers.'

Emerson turned to Rodin. Rodin turned to me, then to DP.

'We'll get into this in more detail later, but you didn't catch anything unusual on the console before the program went down – no unusual readings, no interruptions, nothing?'

'Just the power surge before everything went black. Other than that, I saw nothing.'

Rodin nodded, giving DP the once over. His suspicion

unsettled me. I guess it was his job. He turned to me.

'Agent Zervas, you were the one inside when it went down. Emerson told me about the old man that interrupted the operation – can you tell me any more about that?'

'Yeah, the target's grandfather, I assume. We didn't think it was anything out of the ordinary.'

'But he tried to hand you a letter?'

'Yeah. Took it from his pocket and tried to hand it to me.'

'Anything strange about this letter, did you see who it was addressed to? Was it meant for you, perhaps?'

'To the best of my knowledge, the envelope was blank.'

'Uh-huh. And when things went dark, what then?'

'Things went dark. I found myself in a black hole. The ground underfoot was like flesh. I was naked. I tried to walk out of there, following what sounded like a heartbeat, and finally came upon a wall. A fleshy wall. I tried to climb through it and that's when DP picked up my signal and pulled me out of there.'

'That's it? Nothing else strange or untoward?'

'Nothing,' I said.

Rodin nodded, not taking his eyes from me. Then he turned to Deen.

'We'll want to run some tests obviously,' Deen said. 'You mind if we do a deep dive and see if we can't recover anything from your subconscious?'

'Mind if we wait a day?' I turned to Emerson. 'Like you said, we're pretty frazzled.'

Emerson nodded. 'Give him a day. We don't want to provoke any physical stress while he's under.'

Deen nodded.

'Okay. Thank you, gentlemen. We'll talk again.' Rodin nodded to us then turned to Emerson. 'If that's all, sir...'

'You go ahead, gentlemen. Let me know if there's anything else you need.'

Rodin left and Deen followed. I looked at DP, then turned to the large steel clock on the wall behind Emerson. It was four o'clock. I'd been up since eight the night before.

'You look tired, both of you. Go home and get some rest.'

'Thank you sir.' DP pushed back his seat and stood up. He stretched.

I nodded. 'Yes sir.'

'And gentlemen – stay vigilant.'

'Bit of a shitshow, huh?' DP said to me when we were below in the car park.

'Yeah. Sure is.' I looked away. I was zapped.

'You wanna grab breakfast?'

'Breakfast? It's almost dinner time.'

He shrugged. 'You know the story.'

'Nah,' I said. 'I wanna get to bed. I'm wrecked.'

'Yeah sure. Alright. See you in a day or two.' He turned and walked away. I stood there until he was in his car and driving away. He tooted the horn as he pulled out. I got in the car, shut the door, and sat there for a bit. I had a pretty ragged sense of apprehension hanging on me. It may just have been the lack of sleep, but there was also that big fucking lie I'd dropped in the meeting. And now they wanted to go digging.

I shook my head. 'Fucking idiot.'

I started up the car and drove out of the car park and up into the street above.

It was a gray, listless afternoon. As tired as I was, I didn't think I could face the empty apartment and the bed. So I drove, no particular destination in mind, just doing laps of the city, up and down the busy streets of the center. It was about twenty minutes in I noticed a car on my tail. Or it seemed like it. A brown sedan two cars back, and no matter what way I turned, it stayed with me. And I was driving like someone with dementia. Maybe it figured I was onto it, because it turned the opposite way from me as I was passing the park for the second time, but five minutes later it was back on my tail, this time three cars back. I got spooked. I turned toward the ring road to take me back toward the old stadium. It was on the edge of an industrial park and the roads were quieter out there. As I took the slip road for the park, the sedan flew on by, not turning after me. I tried to get a look at the driver but the windows were tinted.

I pulled up at the cantina and sat in the car and watched the road, waiting to see if the sedan would return. When it didn't, I got out and went inside and took a booth by the window. I watched. The waitress came and I ordered a plate and a beer. The cantina was half-empty and the patrons ate quietly. A few outliers like me, drifters with the mark of solitude about them. One or two men who ate together but silently. No women, only the waitress.

She brought the food and put it in front of me wordlessly.

'Gracias,' I said.

Then I ate. I wasn't particularly hungry but my body felt like it needed it. All the while, one eye on the road outside. The car never returned. When I was done eating, I drank. The beer calmed my shattered nerves.

'Otra vez?' the waitress said when the bottle was drained.

'No gracias.'

I sat there until my eyes began to close. No more putting it off, I needed to sleep. I got up and went to take a piss. I stood at the lavatory in a daze. A few seconds standing there and the writing scrawled in scratchy letters on the wall came into focus: *A la mierda el sistema.*

I zipped up and left.

6

Analytics was a sterile place: pale blue walls, white ceiling, eight desks split into two islands of four. At the back of the department the observation room, which was a room with an insertion point, the glass a one-way mirror which doubled as a console, so that one could observe an agent's biochemical responses as well as watch operational events. Pretty high-tech stuff, but then Vathos was a prestigious operation. The whole department was also immaculately clean.

'This should have been done days ago, Agent Zervas, but what with everything going on, we just haven't had the time. Do we need to run through protocol again?'

'No.'

'Good. Then I'm gonna patch you in.'

Gottfried wired me up with the epidural and I relaxed into the chair.

'What did you score on your last appraisal, do you remember?' he asked.

'Mid-eighties, I think.'

'Hmm. Alright. Then this should be no problem. We'll start off slow then ramp it up bit by bit. You know the drill.'

'Sure.'

'I'm dropping you in.'

There was a searing sideways flash then darkness. When

I heard his voice again, it was through the dense fog of the Structure.

—You're in.

'Yeah. I'm in residual.'

I looked around at the vast desert of my subconscious.

—I'm loading an intro program. Here we go.

I felt the surge through my cerebral cortex and closed my eyes, and when I opened them I was lying on a reclining bed next to a pool. I looked around. Seemed I was in a spa retreat center of some kind.

'This is nice,' I said.

—Just warming you up.

'Keep it up.'

I put my hands behind my head and relaxed. I checked out the patrons that lounged around the pool to make sure there were no familiar faces. Reassured, I relaxed. A soft music drifted over the pool area; at the south side, a man and woman sat under a massaging waterfall. Looked painful. I felt like jumping into the water. I stood up, but a woman appeared at my shoulder and addressed me.

'Mr. Zervas? We're ready for your appointment.'

I looked at her and paused.

—Just go with it, Gottfried said in my ear.

The woman held out her hand. I smiled and took it. She turned and led me away.

I followed her through a door into a hallway. We stopped at a door halfway down and she took me inside and closed the door. In the room was a massage table.

'We don't do breakfast in low-season,' she said.

'I'm sorry?'

'I said you may get undressed.'

'Alright.'

I slipped out of my shorts and lay on the bed, belly down. I put my head on my arms.

She spoke as she busied herself with the oils on the table. 'Have you been raped before?'

'Fuck did you say?'

'I said, are you suffering from any past traumas, anything that may be released under massage?'

'You're not helping to relax me,' I said.

'Our goal is not relaxation, Mr. Zervas, you know that. Our goal is analysis.'

'Yeah, I know. Just go easy on me, alright?'

'I love you, cherubim.'

'What?'

'This will not hurt. I promise.'

I tilted my head to see she was naked. She lifted a bottle of oil and poured it over her breasts, then over my back. Then she climbed on top of me.

'Oh shit,' I whispered.

She lay down and slid over me, gently. I felt the first stirrings of sexual excitement. Her hands were on my shoulders, on my back, in my hair. Her long hair tickled my cheek as she slid upward, and drifted over my shoulders as she slid down over my body, massaging me with her breasts. I breathed deeply and closed my eyes. Where was this goin—?

A searing pain tore at my neck and I screamed. I reached back, taking a handful of her hair.

'You bitch!' I screamed. I pulled, sending her over my shoulder to the floor. Her teeth ripped at my skin as they were pulled from my neck. I slid off the bed and gripped her hair before she could get to her feet, and flung her against the wall. A chunk of her hair remained in my hand. When she raised her head again, she was holding a rock lamp. Like a cat, she leapt at me, swinging at the same time to catch me on the temple with the sharp edge of the lamp. I felt my head split open and blood filled my left eye. When she lunged again, I swung the small stand holding the oils at her, catching her on the chin and dropping her to the floor. I jumped on her, pinning her to the ground. She snarled at me, two long incisors dripping with my blood protruding from her open mouth.

I punched her once, twice… then with a kind of twist, she

got a leg around my neck and spun, sending me head over heels across the floor. I looked up in time to see her spring, and I raised my hand with the broken oil bottle in time to force it into her neck. She squealed. I gripped her hair and pulled her head down onto the broken glass. Her blood washed over me.

When the light went out in her eyes, I pushed her off me and onto the blood-soaked floor.

I stood up.

'Vampires, Gottfried? Are you fucking kidding me?'

—One of my colleagues must have been feeling creative.

'Fuck this,' I said.

—You're doing very well, Agent Zervas. Hang in there.

There was a knock on the door and it opened. A man in a white coat stood there. He looked at the girl on the floor and then at me.

'You look a little cut up, Mr. Zervas. Why don't you come with me and I'll get you fixed up?'

'I'm not sure I want to,' I said.

—You know the drill Agent Zervas, Gottfried said.

I took a deep breath. My forehead was still gushing with blood. 'Fine. Let's go.'

Naked and bloody, I followed the doctor out of the room and down the hall, and we stepped out into the garden. Crossing the patio we set out across the lawn. In the middle of the lawn was a glass elevator. The doctor pushed a button and the doors opened.

'Fuck's sake,' I said.

I followed him in. The doors shut. My heart was racing.

—Control yourself, Agent Zervas.

'I'm fucking trying.'

The lift descended. As soon as it was below ground level, it went dark. My stomach tensed up and I covered my cock and balls with my hands instinctively. The lift was absolutely silent; I couldn't even be sure the doctor was still in there with me.

It started as a tickle. Then a sharp pain. Seconds later, I had a feeling like some barbed weed was crawling into my ear. I spun around, but no matter what way I turned, I couldn't stop it. It went further, deeper, getting thicker as it slithered in. The barbs tore at the inside of my head and I howled.

The lift stopped and the lights came on. When I opened my eyes I was lying on the floor, alone in the lift. The doors opened. Standing on the other side was the doctor.

'You sick fucks,' I said.

'Come with me please, Mr. Zervas.'

I stood up, hands still clasped about my head. The searing pain inside had stopped. I stepped out of the lift.

I followed the doctor into a lecture theater. It was packed with medical staff. Their faces were masked, their eyes closed. The doctor instructed me to get into the reclining chair in the middle of the theater. Two other doctors stood to the side.

'This is not gonna be pleasant, is it?' I said.

'Nothing to worry about, Mr. Zervas. It's all standard procedure.'

'Procedure, yeah…'

I lay back in the chair and he restrained me at the wrists and ankles.

'I want you to feel relaxed, Mr. Zervas. Do you feel relaxed?'

'Oh yeah. I feel relaxed. Super relaxed.'

'Good.' He patted my arm and smiled. 'Let's get you cleaned up.'

The doctor waved to the two other medical staff and they lifted cotton swabs and disinfectant, and stood on either side of me. They proceeded to dab out my wounds with care. When they were finished, they applied lotion to the cuts and bruises and bandaged them.

'How does that feel, hmm? Better?'

'Very thoughtful of you, Doctor. I feel much better. I don't suppose you're gonna turn me loose now, huh?'

'I suppose we better check your insides too. While you're here – don't you think?'

'Actually, I'd rather you didn't…'

The doctor turned to the table, and lifted a jar and rested it between my legs. It was full of black worms. He unscrewed the lid, then turned to the crowd in the theater.

'New advances in medical technology have ensured we have greater insight into the inner workings of human physiology than at any point in history. We're now gifted with the ability to cure human ills without even opening up the body. And it took no more investment than the breeding of some of the oldest organisms on this very planet…'

He dipped his hand into the jar and lifted out two of the worms. He dropped them on my belly.

'Doctor…'

'Don't you worry about a thing…'

They squirmed on my torso for a second and then parted, one crawling toward my belly button, the other toward my nipple. The first slid right inside my belly button. I felt it slither through my skin.

'Uh, *fuck no*…'

I looked at the ceiling and closed my eyes. Breathed. I was trained for this.

The other burrowed under right below my nipple.

'Do you see?' The doctor was addressing the hall. 'Remarkable what a few simple organisms can do in only a couple of seconds.'

I opened my eyes to see him lift another from the jar. He dropped it on my thigh.

'Sweet Jesus,' I whispered.

It slid up the inside of my thigh toward my crotch. My skin crawled. Fingers stretching taut, I tested the tightness of the straps. They held me fast.

The worm burrowed into the flesh where the thigh met my body. I gritted my teeth, my lips dry and taut.

'We can even target the more specialized parts of the body,' the doctor continued, and he picked up another and dropped it on my face.

'No, no…' It slithered over my cheek and I felt it at my

nostril, but it stopped and turned and slid toward my eye. One of the medical assistants took my head in her hands. 'Get it off me...'

It pushed in under the eyelid. I felt every little bristle on my eyeball as it pushed through my eye socket into my head. My whole body contorted, I struggled not to scream. My gut was in spasm.

I fought down the terror. The things were still writhing inside me. My asshole was clenched tight and my hands were like claws. I was frothing at the mouth.

When the discomfort passed, there was a sinister applause from the audience.

'Marvelous, how the human body can heal itself,' said the doctor. 'It's a landscape we'll never fully discover, nor appreciate in its entirety. Of course, there are some ills that we simply need to extract the old-fashioned way.'

I heard the whirr of a blade and tilted my head to see a surgical saw in his hand. I grimaced.

'Even to this very day, our core diseases are those which we foster and create for ourselves. Psychosomatosis is the first and greatest enemy of all humans, and one which we have scarce learned to command...'

He started up the circular saw and lowered it to my chest, and began an autopsy Y-cut from each of my shoulder blades to my sternum. Blood shot from the incision. I fought with the straps but I was going nowhere. My grinding teeth sounded like screeching metal. Saliva frothed in my mouth. Then he began the cut to my navel. As soon as he passed over my belly button, fingers pushed out of my stomach. Then the hands.

'What the *fuck*...'

Arms. Then a head. When a young me pushed his way out of my stomach, that's when I passed out.

7

'You did very well, considering,' Gottfried said.

'What was the score?'

'A few points down, but given the events of the past few days, I doubt anyone'll complain.'

I sat up, flexed my neck, closed my eyes and took a deep breath.

'Emerson suggested we attempt the retrieval while you're down here. It was a rough session, but do you mind hanging around for a bit? Better to get it out of the way…'

'Sure.' I sighed. 'But maybe give me a half-hour in rec before I go under?'

Gottfried waved a hand. 'Sure. That goes without saying. We need you relaxed.'

'Good.' I got up and put on my hoodie. 'I'll see you in a bit.'

'I'll be here.'

I went out of Analytics and up to the third floor. Third floor was where the staff communal areas were – a small canteen, a break room, some meeting rooms and a recreational area. Recreation was equipped with VR consoles so staff could relax in any number of scenarios while off-duty. Before going into VR I went into the bathroom at the end of a hall and into a cubicle, locking the door. I took the hypodermic from my pocket and slipped the cover off the needle. Pushing down my pants, I pinched the skin of my thigh and plunged the needle in.

When I was done, I went out and into the rec room.

'A pleasant half-hour?' Gottfried asked when I went back down to Analytics.

'I didn't spend it in the spa, I can tell you that much,' I said.

'No. I guess not.'

I climbed into the chair.

'Well, let's see if we can recover anything useful from your memories,' he said.

Gottfried plugged in the epidural and I relaxed into the chair. He sat at the console.

'Nothing too intrusive – we're just going to have a little poke around.'

'Sure.'

There was the flash, and I closed my eyes and opened them in the dark. Gottfried dropped me into residual with a night overlay, and I sat down on the warm sands of my subconscious mental landscape.

—I'm gonna roll back the chronology of the past few days, but you know how fickle the mind is with time, so please be patient.

'Sure. Take your time.'

The landscape around me morphed, brightened and darkened again, then bushes grew up around me and grass underneath, and I realized I was sitting in a chair in the tiny park in front of the courthouse.

'You've gone too far.'

—Ah. Forgive me.

The scene flickered and the house from the mission materialized around me, except I found myself sitting on the settee in front of grandma.

'We're almost there,' I said. 'Except everything's a little off, somehow. Not quite to spec.'

—Strange. Gottfried rolled things forward. I saw a flash

of the boy in the bed and the spike in my hand, then I was sitting in that vast clammy landscape again that stretched in all directions. I heard the faint intonations of classical music.

'Yeah, this is it. Except there's music. There was no music.'

—Hmm. Things are fuzzy. I'm applying a few filters.

The music died, and once again I heard the echo of a heartbeat.

'That's more like it,' I said.

—Okay. So what now?

'So I followed the sound of the heartbeat…' I stood up and looked around me.

—Mm-hmm.

'You'll need to be quiet for a moment, Gottfried. I need to identify the source.'

—Yes. Sorry.

He fell silent and I turned slowly to find the source of the heartbeat. When it was clear, I walked off in the direction of the sound.

'Okay. I have it. I don't know how long I walked, I just know that I hit a wall at some point.'

—Okay. I'll be quiet until you get there.

I walked. The dreamscape was much as before. Only the occasional leakage made it clear I was in a recollection: a brief and shadowy figure I thought was an old landlady of mine, the purring of her cat, the bell of the kitchen in the Mexican cantina, the wall of the cantina toilet…

I reached the wall. 'I'm here,' I said.

—So? What now?

'Then I climbed through…'

—Try it.

I placed my hands on the fleshy wall and pushed. There was give, but it was firmer than before. I told Gottfried.

—Probably normal, given the time that's passed. Maybe you can—

He broke off, hearing the noise. The same noise I was hearing.

—Is that a phone ringing?

'Sounds like it,' I said. 'Wasn't part of the original sequence, though.'

—Where's it coming from?

'From beyond the wall.'

—Try to get to it, Agent Zervas. It's imperative you try to reach that phone.

'I'll try.'

I punched the surface and my hand broke through, but when I tried to extract it, it held fast.

'Something's wrong,' I said.

—What is it?

The wall began to suck me in. Swallow me. The hand, the arm, soon I was in up to my shoulder.

'Something's wrong, Gottfried – this isn't how it went…'

My shoulder disappeared into the wall and I felt the clammy surface close around my neck as my head was sucked in.

'You need to pull me out of here. Now!'

A bright flash. I opened my eyes in the chair, gasping for breath. Gottfried pulled the epidural and put a hand on my arm. My hand went up to my neck where I could still feel the clammy touch of the wall.

'You're out. Everything's fine.'

'I don't know what that was,' I said. 'It wasn't right at all.'

'It's strange. Very strange.' I sat up and he took a seat at the console and punched a few buttons.

'Maybe we ran it too close to the stress test,' I said.

'Maybe.'

I put on my top. 'Well, if there's nothing else, I'd really love to get outta here.'

He turned around. 'Of course, go on. I'll send my report up to Emerson when I've run the analysis.'

I nodded. 'Thanks.'

'Thank you.'

I went out the door, shuddering as I closed it behind me.

On the way home I kept my eyes peeled for the brown sedan. I took a circuitous route out past the stadium and back to the city, and drove down to the Chinese Quarter where it was mostly pedestrianized and parked in a lot behind the Chinese theater. I sat in the car for almost ten minutes, then I got out and stood in front of a tailor's next to the lot and surveyed the street in both directions. When I thought it was safe, I hit the back streets.

It had just gone three and the streets were quiet. I stopped at a food stand and had a bowl of noodles then made my way to the internet café. The café was old school: vintage stacks and beat monitors, and wooden partitioning between the booths. Cruddy headsets worn by generations of street kids. Games posters curling at the edges and the reek of smoke and energy drinks. As I went in the owner nodded and put out a cigarette. I nodded back, sat down.

Internet was forbidden in the homes of agents. We were completely air-gapped and our phones had a rigorous firewall set up around them. The only things coming through were company-vetted. Even sitting here was a breach of my contract worthy of suspension and investigation.

I hit the enter button on the screen. The login screen came up. In Spanish: *Acceder al sistema.* I turned to look at the Chinese guy behind the counter.

'Hey – wanna log me in here?'

He nodded and punched a few buttons on his console. The screen came on. I opened a browser and brought up *Craigslist* and navigated to the *Haiku Hotel* page. Scrolled down.

'Come on, come on... where the fuck are you hiding?' I whispered.

Nothing. A once-a-month ritual that always came to nothing. I sat back in the chair and sighed, then turned to look at the owner who was lighting another cigarette.

'Fuck it.' I got up and dropped a dollar on the counter and nodded. 'Thanks. See ya.'

I went into the street. Nothing for it but to go home.

We were called in that evening for a meeting. The job was coming to a close and Emerson wanted to make sure the final push went smoothly. We sat around a table in one of the operational planning rooms: myself, DP, Maynes, Emerson, Gottfried and Merixel, also from Analytics. Gottfried gave us the theory behind the operation.

'We did a deep dive into the psychology of the mark and came up with a pretty comprehensive picture of his base psychological structures. Despite his asexuality, we see strong indicators that he has, or has had, some pretty ingrained desires to have a normal life, that is, a wife and family and all the rest. Given the strength of these desires, we feel that a dream in which these latent longings were the foundation would be a fitting *pièce de résistance*. In other words, we're going to give him a wife, and then you're going to take her away from him.'

'Let me guess,' I said. 'We're going to take her away in the most gruesome way possible.'

'Of course,' Maynes said, butting in. 'That's what we do here, Zervas. We make nightmares reality.'

I flicked to the page that laid out the dream sequence. 'Oh no, man – this is just fucking twisted. And in a restaurant? On their anniversary?'

Emerson spoke. 'Like Maynes said, we do what we do for maximum psychological damage. The whole point of these operations is to break the individual. This is the quickest way to do it.'

'All I'm saying is, just maybe, subtlety could get the job done as effectively as the hatchet approach. I dunno, maybe he has to watch her fall overboard on a cruise, and watch agonizingly as the ship sails away into the sunset, his wife thrashing in the water below. You know, subtle. And the not knowing—'

'Enough, Zervas,' Emerson said. 'You're way above your paygrade. Everything here is run on probabilities, you know that. And if Analytics says this is the quickest route to getting what we want, then that's what we do.'

Perhaps to help me save face, Merixel spoke up. 'You're idea is good, Agent Zervas, but this kind of trauma works well in the long term. What we want is a shock that's gonna mar his thought processes and critical facilities over the next forty-eight hours. This is the most effective way of doing that.'

'Quick and dirty,' Maynes added. 'If you're not up to the job, say so, and we'll find someone else to take care of it.'

'I'm an agent, sir. I follow orders. Forgive me for speaking out of place.'

Maynes looked at me funny and even DP turned his head to glance at me. Maynes grunted and turned away.

'This is it,' said Emerson. 'The last push. And I don't normally get into client side with operational, it's not your concern, but this is a big client and we want to hold on to them. Success in this job will mean a lucrative few years for us, and I guaran-fucking-tee you I'll be putting you all in for bonuses if this comes off as it should. And I fully expect it to.'

DP clicked his tongue. 'Oh yeah.'

Gottfried cleared his throat. 'One thing I should make clear before you go under – desires like this are deeply rooted and influential in ways which we cannot and will never fully comprehend. Even in a dream they may influence our behavior to a startling degree. That should make us predictable, and in one sense, it does. But when these deep desires are threatened it can also provoke violent reactions. Analeptics will be administering an appropriate cocktail to the target to forestall any adverse reactions to the scenario, but you should be on your guard all the same. Our most fallacious needs are the ones we cling to most desperately.'

'Profound,' said Maynes.

8

'How we lookin', DP?'

'Pretty fucking solid, partner. Pretty fucking solid.'

'Good. Turn down the lights, will ya?'

I closed my eyes as DP fooled around on the console and lowered the lights in the room. You needed it dark to go under. Bright lights weren't conducive to relaxation. He got up and gave me the injection. I flexed my neck.

'Feelin' good?'

'Yeah DP. I'm feeling good.'

'Alright. You just tell me when you're ready.'

'Sure. Go ahead and plug me in. You can set me up in a waiting room for a bit.'

'I hear ya.'

DP plugged in the epidural and sat down at the console. 'Dropping you into residual.'

'Right.'

The flash. I opened my eyes by an oasis.

—Glad to see it's not all barren down there. That's some romantic shit right there.

'Get the fuck outta my happy place DP.'

—Sorry partner. We got a job to do. Who else would hold your hand while we mindfuck a few unfortunates?

'Thank God it's you, DP.'

—You know it. Right, I'm laying a program. Hold onto your seat.

The scene around me shuddered and disappeared, and I found myself in the lobby of a very nice hotel.

—Welcome back to the Structure. Can I get you anything, sir, while you wait?

'Where am I DP?'

—You're in a hotel right across the street from the restaurant. Sit tight while I wait for Sura to get through to me with the go-ahead.

'Sure. Maybe I'll have a drink while I wait.'

—Make sure and order something appropriate to go with that suit.

I looked down at myself. 'Fuck sake.'

—Go on and have a drink, killer. Take the edge off.

Fuck it. Why not. I held up a hand and a waiter came over.

'Whiskey sour,' I said. He nodded and hurried away. I looked around the lobby as I waited. It was populated by an assortment of characters – that's all they were, characters, bit-parts in a scenario being played out in an artificially created mindscape. Beautifully done. I could have sat down and engaged and communicated with any one of them. And while the exchange would certainly have been surreal or at least highly unusual, it would have been authentic. I watched a man in a pin-striped serge suit twirl a pen in his fingers as he watched a woman in a green dress by the hotel entrance. A busboy passed, carrying a case. A receptionist on the phone hailed him over. I turned to see a huge fat lady descend the stairs, every step nearly giving way to an accident.

The waiter returned with my drink and placed it on the coffee table in front of me.

'Sir?'

'Thank you.'

'My mother keeps bees,' he said.

I looked at him and nodded. 'Be sure and tell her to leave water out for the dogs.'

He turned and left.

—Making friends? DP said.

'Oh yeah. Some interesting folk down here.'

—Let's run some tests while you've a drink in your hand.

I sniffed it and took a taste. 'Nothing.'

—Alright. Hey I ever tell you, you put the 'cock' in cocktail, man.

'Fucking eh.' I laughed. I took another sip and cast an eye over the lobby. Right then, a hyena entered through the revolving doors. No one paid any attention. It came over and sniffed the rug beneath my feet, then wandered off toward the restaurant.

—I've got incoming from ground-floor. They're on standby.

'I'm ready when you are.'

—Good. You might wanna go and have a sniff around the restaurant before we go in. But do me a favor and check airtime with that glass before we go.

'Alright.' I took a sip of the whiskey and stood up, and held a hand up to the receptionist, who looked at me and smiled. Then I hurled the glass. Time slowed. The glass drifted through the air with no hurry as I watched, and when it neared the reception it reverted to full speed. The receptionist snatched it from the air and set it down.

—Smooth.

I smiled at the receptionist and nodded. Then I went out into the street.

Right opposite the hotel was Le Havre. French. Of course it was fucking French.

'You ever had escargots, DP?'

—Fuck's that?

'Snails, you dumb shit.'

—The day you catch me eating snails is the day I cut out my own tongue with a pair of rusty scissors.

'Never say never, DP.'

—I've watched you cut off a child's hands, but eating snails? That's going too far.

I grinned. —You are a peculiar one, DP.

—Hold on a minute – ground-floor are applying the epidural. We're just about ready to go.

I stopped by the curb and surveyed the street. Nothing unusual until I looked into the sky and saw an airship. I stepped off the curb and crossed. On the other side, a man approached me.

'Got something to eat?' he said.

I shook my head and reached into my pocket. There was nothing but a packet of cigarettes in there.

'Here,' I said. I handed them to him and he wandered off.

—I didn't know you smoked?

'I don't.'

—Hey, wait up… Okay, we're good to go. You step through those doors and we're operational.

'Fine. I'm going in.'

I went up the steps and opened the door to the restaurant. There was a shimmer in the air, the lights darkening momentarily, then the scene returned to normal. I stepped inside and was met by the maître d'.

'Good evening, sir. Do you have a reservation?'

'Everhill. For one.'

'Right this way sir.' I followed him to a table. 'You're server will be right along.'

'Thank you.'

I sat down and picked up the drinks menu and looked around the restaurant. The walls were a sub-nautical green and graced with large oval mirrors, the tables and chairs black walnut. A single chandelier constructed from wine glasses hung in the center of the room. Soft piano music played. I caught sight of the judge.

—You see him?

'Yeah, I got him.'

—Pretty girl.

'Dream girls always are.'

The judge and his dream wife were sitting in the center

of the restaurant, right under the chandelier. They looked happy. He looked happy. It was their tenth anniversary dinner. She was indeed beautiful, but it was a beauty born of grief and suffering. Something about her seemed out of place.

'Something about her, DP,' I said. 'You sure we designed her like that?'

—What do you mean?

'I don't remember her being so, you know, striking.'

—Fuck's wrong with you? Don't be getting sentimental on me.

I shook my head, dispelling the thought. 'I almost feel bad about spoiling a night like this.'

—Partner, if you're gonna get weird on me, tell me now.

'Nah, I'm just saying – this might be the greatest night of the guy's life, albeit an imaginary one. He's here with his dream woman, feeling like king of the world, and I'm fixing to rape his wife and cut off her head.'

—It's the job, my man. And it's a dream.

'Just sayin'.'

—You've done worse.

I shrugged. 'Maybe. Not in a restaurant though, right? I mean, all the time we've worked together, have I done some shit like this in public?'

—Does it matter?

'Yeah, it kinda does.'

—How?

'Well listen to me DP, it's all very well if you're with the woman you love at home on the sofa, but would you take her down the beach and fuck her on a greasy beach bed in front of a hundred strangers?'

—Why not?

'You fucking heathen.'

A waiter appeared with a bottle of red wine, opened it and poured me a glass. I tasted it and nodded. He left.

—And besides, this isn't the woman you love.

'I know. But isn't rape an intimate act too?'

69

—How, you fucking lunatic? And need I remind you that this conversation is on record. This job goes south, this could all be a black mark against you.

'Fuck it, DP, don't give me that shit. We're just spitballin' til things get rolling. Look, all I'm saying is, any kind of... *congress* between two people, is intimate, whether it's forced or not. Rapists operate in the dark, not in public.'

—Which is why it's going down like this. Can you imagine the mindfuck from seeing your wife violated in public?

'Yeah. Still. I'd prefer a hotel room.'

—Well ain't that just too fucking bad. Boo-hoo.

The lights of the chandelier flickered. 'Something up, DP?'

'Don't think so, partner. Any second now he's gonna pull out that necklace and you're gonna get up and put it on her.'

'DP, where's my hatchet?'

—Oh shit...

A hatchet materialized on the table in front of me.

—Bit of a slip.

I slid my hand around the handle and picked it up. Tested its weight. The waiter returned to the table.

'Are you ready to order?'

'I need ten more minutes,' I said. He nodded and left.

I put the hatchet down.

—Heads up, partner...

'What is it?'

—Maynes is here.

'Maynes? What the fuck is Maynes doing here?'

His voice came in my ear. —Been some changes, Zervas. Last minute.

'Changes? What changes?'

—We've altered the sequence. You're not gonna rape her and cut off her head. You're gonna cut off her head then rape her.

'What? No I'm not. I'm gonna do what was in the brief – you know, the thing we've been working toward this last forty-eight hours.'

—Zervas, now listen to me. This is a sanctioned chang—

'It's a breach of protocol is what it is, Maynes. And I'm not fucking doing it.'

—Listen to me, fuckstick. This has been OK'd at the highest level, from Emerson's desk itself. Now, you gonna do what's needed or do I need to come down there?

'DP, you let that monkey into my job and I'll bounce you off the four walls…'

—Right, put me in…

'DP…'

—Nothing I can do partner. Security's here.

'For fuck's sake…'

I stood up and lifted the hatchet off the table, and walked toward the couple. Before I'd reached the center of the room, Maynes grabbed my arm from a chair as I passed.

'Fuck are you doing in here?' I said.

'Stopping you from fucking up this operation.'

'You asshole…'

I swung at him but he side-stepped it and caught me with a fist in the ribs, taking my breath. I countered with a right elbow to his jaw and sent him reeling, then brought the back of the hatchet across his knee. He buckled, but threw his weight at me and brought me to the ground. His hand was on my wrist, restraining the hatchet, his knee on my stomach. I looked up at his fat, furious face.

'You've been waiting for this, haven't you?' I said.

'You're fucking right I have.' He brought his other knee down on my forearm, forcing me to release the hatchet. He snatched it up. 'You're a goddamned liability, Zervas.'

He swung the hatchet at my head.

I opened my eyes in the chair, immediately turning to see Maynes in the chair next to me. I reached behind me and pulled the epidural.

'I'll fucking kill him,' I said, leaping from the chair. Security was on me in a second.

'Don't,' DP said. 'You'll just make it worse…'

9

'Can I come in?'

Roche peered through the crack in the door. 'You don't have an appointment.'

'Do I need one?'

She regarded me for a moment before opening up. I stepped in past her.

'I'm not working on you.'

'That's not why I'm here.'

She closed the door and locked up, and I followed her into the studio where she picked up a joint that sat smoldering in the ashtray. The Ramones played low on her sound system. She sat down, puffed on the joint and eyed me.

'Are you sitting?'

'I dunno.' I looked around at the tats on the wall. Roses, skulls, Chinese symbols. I pointed at one. 'What does that mean?'

She flicked the ash. 'It means, sit the fuck down and don't be rude.'

'Hmm.' I took off my jacket but didn't sit.

'Here, take this.'

She handed me the joint. I took it and smoked, and exhaled violently.

'You had a bad day.'

'You could say that.'

She sighed and stood up, and pulled off her T-shirt. 'Fine. Take off your clothes.'

When we were done she opened a bottle of whiskey and poured two glasses and handed me one. I sipped it and looked into the glass.

'Whatever you're looking for, you won't find it in there.'

'Agh.' I drained the glass and put it on the floor. 'I know.' I put my arms behind my head. 'You ever go out?' I said.

'What do you mean?'

'I mean, are you always stuck inside these four walls?'

'I'm not a hermit. I go out.'

'Where do you go?'

She waved a hand and said nothing, as if that was all the answer I needed to my dumb questions.

'I thought I saw you last week in the Chinese Quarter.'

'Why – because I'm Chinese and Chinese people can only go to the Chinese Quarter?'

'No.' I held my hand out for the joint she'd just lit. 'Because I see ghosts. Everywhere I go.'

'Am I haunting you?'

'Not yet.' I took a draw on the joint and handed it back.

'I'm sure you have lots of ghosts. One more won't hurt you.' She lay back so that we were both looking at the ceiling. The paint was yellow with age and speckled with what could have been blood, or perhaps it was the result of one listless night's attempt at something artistic, with paint lashed with abandon into the air. Whatever it was, it did not look out of place. I turned, and slid a hand down over her belly onto her sex. She was warm and wet. Her face did not register my touch.

'Don't you have ghosts?' I said.

'No.'

'Why?'

'Because I don't do what you do.'

'How do you know what I do?'

'Even a blind man could see what you do.' Her little finger was tracing a line back and forth over her upper lip, the butt between her fingers emitting a slow trace of smoke ceilingward.

'Nah, you don't know what I do.'

She didn't take the bait. And I couldn't just come out and ask. I slipped a finger inside her and put my mouth to her tit. I caught a playful smile on her lips.

'What?'

She shook her head. 'Stop asking questions. If you're gonna come around here, you don't ask questions. That's the deal.'

'Jesus.'

'There is a better use for your mouth,' she said. She pushed my head toward her sex.

I fixed up my boots and put on my jacket, and when I was ready for leaving, Roche reached up to her bookshelf and lifted something down. I held up a hand to forestall her.

'Don't be giving me any books please. I don't nee—'

'I'm not giving you my book.' She opened it and took out a small card, and handed it to me. 'You have a particular kind of darkness in you tonight. Only one thing will take it away. Here…'

She handed me the card.

'What's this?'

'Go and see him. You need it.'

I looked at the card. It was no more than an address. Chinese Quarter by the looks of it.

'Is this some crack den, Roche?'

'That would not help you either.'

I slipped it into my pocket. 'Alright.' I nodded. 'Hey, thank—'

'Go,' she said.

'Yeah. I'm going. See you.' I opened the door and went out into the alley. I heard the door lock behind me. Two KPs were at the back door of the restaurant kitchen and looked at me strangely as I headed toward the street.

'Hey, you have a light buddy?' one said.

I shook my head. 'Sorry.'

At the end of the alley I turned right into the street and got in my car. Home seemed like a daunting prospect. I took the card from my pocket and checked the address.

'You gotta be fucking crazy…'

I started the car and took off.

The place was on an alley on the other side of the fish market nestled between a mobile phone store and a launderette. Aluminum and locked from the inside, I hammered on the door. The noise resounded in the quiet alley. It was almost a minute before it was answered by a guy in a vest with full-sleeve tattoos. He shrugged his shoulders and tilted his head quizzically.

'What do you want, pal?'

I held up the card. He gestured me inside with a tilt of his head, slamming the door and locking it behind me.

'Come with me.' He started down the stairs.

'Hold on a minute,' I said. 'What do you do here?'

He turned. 'If you don't know why you're here you're in the wrong place, pal.' His accent was heavy Scottish.

I shook my head. 'Nah, I'm in the right place. Let's go.'

He regarded me carefully before turning and walking down the stairs. I followed. The stairs led onto a short corridor illuminated by tube lighting, at the end of which was a door. He led me inside.

I saw the chairs and I'd an inkling right away what the deal was. There were six of them arranged around a master tower, the epidurals all hooked up to the central stack. There was one other man on a seat on the chair furthest from me, the epidural connected to the base of his skull and he lost in whatever corner of the metaconsciousness he'd paid to be transported to. I turned to see the guy with the tattoos sit at a console. I stepped up behind him.

'What are you offering here?'

'Whatever your needs require, pal. We got Junkie, Celestial, mindwash, brainbreaks, barbies, Marquis de Sade, womb reversion, fairytales, total and absolute sensory deprivation, sensory drowning, Up-the-ladder-and-down-the-slide, Mind Rotator, Patricide, Godhead, Metalhead, Buff Logic, Cranial Limbo... you name it, we got it. Fuck sake, if you just wanna take a wee ride on the choo-choo up the Scottish Highlands, I'll do that for you too.' He looked at me over his shoulder and winked.

'You recommend anything?'

'First time?'

'In the chair? No.'

'Ah. Well in that case, if I'm gettin' the vibes I think I'm gettin', I might go for a mindwash or a wee bit of Godhead. What do you say? Godhead sound good?'

'What's that?'

'What's the best blowjob you ever had in your life?' Before I could answer he rattled on. 'Well, take that and multiply it by a thousand, and then imagine God blowing softly over your erection – except the erection is your *mind*, pal. That sound like it might float your boat?'

I took off my jacket.

'Five hundred a pop, partner. But you get the best part of two hours for that.'

I nodded. 'You take cash?'

'We only take cash.'

I took a roll of dirty bills and unfurled them, peeling off five and handing them to him.

'Good man. Take a wee seat right over there. By the way – is your phone switched off?'

'Yes.'

He nodded.

I lay back in the chair and exhaled. Nerves were clawing at the edges of my mind, but I'd come this far and was committed. I clenched my fist as the guy sat and loaded up the program then got up again. He went to a fridge and took out a vial. Then he opened a drawer. With relief I saw him take out a disposable needle. He put on a pair of latex gloves and opened the hypodermic.

'Do I need to know what's in that?' I said as he plunged the needle into the vial.

'No you do not.'

'I work in the business. I get tested once a week.'

'Will you get tested tomorrow?'

'No.'

'Good. It'll be out of your system in twenty-four hours, my man.'

He put the needle in my arm. I felt an immediate warmth and my body found the comfort of the chair. I let go. Barbiturates in the cocktail for sure.

'I hope you sterilize the epidurals,' I said.

He shook his head and turned to another drawer. He opened it and took out a small thin package. 'No need. We use disposable.'

'Where do you get those?' I said.

'Now now. That would be telling. Sit forward.' I sat up and he attached the epidural to the cable and placed it on the back of my neck. He pushed me gently back into the seat. 'Right-o, pal. Let's set you sailin', shall we?'

He sat at the console. 'Right then. Settle in and we'll get you in the air. Let's see now, what did we say – barbies, was it?'

'Godhead.'

He turned and winked. 'Only kiddin' ya. I got ya. Don't you worry, I got ya...'

I looked at the console, at the all-too-familiar dual screen, one with the stats and biochemical analysis, and one for a rough rendition of the programmed mindscape. I wouldn't see it, but soon it would display whatever dream reality I'd be programmed into.

'Wait – you're not harvesting any data here are you?' I said.

He turned and shook his head. 'We don't do that here, pal.

Certainly not with the likes of you.'

I nodded.

'Alright then. If you've no further questions, I'm dropping you in.'

I was already fighting my eyelids which sought only to close, so I shut them and let myself go. There was a searing flash and I was pulled in, coming around in a vast turquoise-blue expanse... not exactly in it, because I was no longer 'in' it, I was part of it, enmeshed into the ethereal fabric of space and time and space-time, extending in all directions and without limit or end.

The operator spoke: —I'm only gonna interrupt once then I'm gonna shut up. It probably goes without saying for the likes of yourself, but if at any time you need to eject, just say the word. But I don't foresee any problems.

'Fine.'

He logged off, and I drowned in a sublime silence that was like the birth of everything. An eternal endless whisper that was soundless and without sound yet composed of everything, and a wind like a torrential breeze that held me aloft and which swam around me in undulating waves of extreme serene, the essence of me beholden to it and composed of it and it contained within me too, for there was no division between the universal elements and the particles and the atoms, and the things that were constructed thereof, the breeze heavier than that which I was, the all-things-that-are-which-are-not, in other words nameless, for in the eternal emptiness of the mind there's no need for semiotics.

I revolved, and my perception gave rise to the evolution of my being, and I opened my eyes to find I was sitting on a cloud, in front of me a great peacock. It gazed into me for a long time then spread its feathers and shook, and angels tiny and innumerable were shaken from the fronds of its plumage and they floated into the sky like fireflies, each one of them whispering a golden song which made my atoms vibrate and which caused a kind of elemental fission in me, and the songs released the heaviness from my atomic structure so that I heard the song of my own essence, and it was no different from that of the angels. The thousandeyed peacock unfurled his plumage over me like a shawl. Around me it became dark and I saw only the radiant eyes of the peacock's coat; each one stared into me so deeply that I saw I was nothing and contained nothing, no matter the memories or the desires or the fears or hopes, it was all nothing under the eternal eye. The eye was and I was not, and the song was and the atom was not, and the angels were and would always be and only for that I was not a ghost alone in the machine, the great machine that was the unhappy illusion of particles and prisons and earthly lore, the great emptiness, the undulating reams of eternal illusion, but that illusion has no part of the essence of man and I saw it and understood. Decanted into me then like a great downpouring of warm rain was all that was not illusion, the substance that sustains and is invisible and unknown to us but to which we owe our being, for without it there is nothing, even in the very bones of us, and the downpour teased apart my fears and my designs and my terrors and dreams, they dissolving in the deluge that was the shower of God, and when I'd been washed clean of earthly mind all that was left was soul. The soul of me drifted through a blue wilderness uncluttered with the affairs of men, not even their dreams, and in that blue desert I came to a kind of gate, a gate that was only the reflection of itself and therefore no gate at all, but the passing through it was clear to me and I knew on the other side lay what men call heaven, but heaven is nothing but the dissolution of all matter, real and ethereal, which means giving up also one's soul. Here it was – the Godhead. Pass and enter the realm of the Maker, the font, the wellspring…

I could not. I turned and drifted through that blue desert until I came across an oasis which was for the souls who were not ready to let go. I sank into the empyreal waters of the oasis, swimming in the abortive souls of others like me, and in that was the power that those like me sought – to penetrate, to subvert, to pollute. There we swam, all of us, souls innumerable beyond the material, engorged on the essence of each other. Some were vast, some were ghosts, some were legion. Some sang and some whispered, some trembled and some raged. Some came apart, and some were condensed as grains of sand. All of us souls were souls apart and one at the same time and I knew in my essence that it would always be, and in that was heaven but hell also, for heaven and hell were conjoined and one and would be evermore. So I let myself drown in the eternal oasis of souls, and therein I found nothing and everything, just as on earth, and therein was the essence of the Godhead.

After an age, I opened my eyes and found myself back in the dirty basement. I looked up to see the guy on the console watching porn. He tilted his head as if he'd heard me move and spoke over his shoulder.

'How was heaven?'

I shook my head. I was still foggy and couldn't speak.

'A trip, huh?' He put down the chips he was eating and turned. 'I still remember my first stint in the Godhead. Man, my mind was like goo for a week. Shit. Hey, you just take your time there. No rush. Get your head straight before you try and get up.'

I turned my head. A chair two places over was occupied by a girl who hadn't been there when I'd come in.

The guy leaned toward me. 'You won't believe the shit this chick is into. I'm telling you… fucking *crazy*. Wanna watch?'

'No.' I tried to sit forward but was still attached to the epidural.

'Hey, hold on there…'

He got up, came over and unplugged me. I stood up.

'You probably don't wanna be running out of here in such a hurry, pal.'

'I'll be fine.'

'Alright. Your shout.'

I walked toward the door and up the stairs. He followed. When we got to the top of the stairs, he unlocked the door and I stepped outside.

'You come back and see us anytime, my man, you hear?' He winked and closed the door. I stood in the light sprinkling of rain that fell. I looked skyward, my mind still somewhat in that dreamspace, the rain almost falling through me, through my body. At least that's how it felt.

I looked around, unsure for a moment where I was. Driven by some inner compass, I started walking. The streets were dark and lit only by intermittent neon lights that advertised the seedy businesses above whose doors they hung. The neon sparkled on the white streets which I wound my way along. It was quiet out, but I heard televisions and voices through windows, arguments and laments and laughter, the sounds and the lights a mere backdrop to the mindscape through which I still walked.

Arriving back at the main road, I stopped in front of the empty space where my car had been parked. Unsure if I was in a glitch of some kind, I slipped my hand into my jacket pocket and took out my car keys, and stared at them for a minute. I looked back at the empty space.

'Fuck,' I whispered, suddenly pulled back into cold reality. 'Son of a bitch.' I looked up and down the street and saw no one. I took out my phone, realizing I'd turned it off. 'Jesus fucking Christ.'

I turned the phone on and was waiting for it to boot when I heard a car round the corner and looked up. It was a taxi. Shoving the phone in my pocket, I stepped out into the road and held out a hand. The car slowed, approaching cautiously, and came to a stop next to me. I looked up at the soft rain before I opened the door and hopped in the back. The guy at the wheel said nothing.

'Everley,' I said.

He nodded and pulled away. I ran my hand through my hair. It felt strangely lush. I turned to look out the window, the night soft and surreal. My phone buzzed with new messages, and I extracted it from my pocket to glance at the screen then shoved it back inside.

The driver took a turn south heading toward the highway.

'Hey, where you going?' I said. He was silent and I knocked on the glass. 'Hey…'

I looked out the window then and saw the billboard that towered above the side of the road. It spoke to something inside me.

'Stop the car!' I shouted and the car came to a halt. I got out. I went into my pocket to grab a bill but the driver pulled off. 'Hey!'

He was gone. I looked up at the billboard.

ENTRAR EL SISTEMA

Some bland advertisement for a gym, but the words…

I turned to look down the alley next to me which retreated into darkness. Compelled by what, I had no idea, but I glanced up at the billboard once more before stepping into the alley.

A cat purred somewhere. That was the only sound I heard as I went other than the tap of the rain on the steel steps above my head. I had no idea what I was looking for. I heard a noise behind me and stopped and turned. There was nothing, no one. I continued down the alley to a nondescript door on the left, on it a nondescript sign:

Sistema de seguridad en funcionamiento

The word 'sistema' was in red and everything else black. Without a second thought I stepped forward and knocked. It was answered.

Struck dumb, I merely stared at her as she opened the door. I shook my head.

'You…'

She raised a Faraday bag and opened it and held it out. The woman from the dream. The judge's dream wife. I stared, mouth open.

'Your phone,' she said.

I shook my head. 'How…?'

She stared at me coldly. 'Give me your phone.'

I put my hand in my pocket and took it out.

She gestured with an urgent tilt of the head. 'Get in off the street. Now.'

CONTINUE WITH PART TWO...

Acolyte

Caleb, a young school dropout, robs an apartment one night with his petty-criminal friend, Vince. Finding an expensive and rare piece of computer hardware, he pockets it, oblivious to its power and purpose. The boy plugs himself into the new device, unaware that the program inside it is a diabolical piece of software, one which almost kills him. But those who created the program do not want it out in the world and will do anything to retrieve it, including killing anyone in whose possession it is found. Caleb may find that by taking the device he has unwittingly unleashed forces that will consume all he knows and loves.

Chimera

Following the murder of her young son, Celeste goes all in with a group of co-conspirators to infiltrate Vathos, the company she believes responsible for the death of her child. The faction make tentative contact with Vangelis Zervas, hoping he will help them penetrate the Vathos servers so they may gather evidence to bring the company down. Despite the nature of his ruthless and horrific work, Vangelis may have his own misgivings with the company. But is it enough for him to turn on Vathos?

In the end, he may have only one choice: Hell or death.

LITTLE SWINE

A small basement cell. A dirty bed. A chair.

These are the confines of Little Swine's world. Prisoner of Momma and subject to the tortures of Boy, her life is a living hell.

Momma has a plan. Momma wants a baby that she may redeem the sins of her past. This is Little Swine's purpose. And when Momma has what she wants, Little Swine will be discarded.

But violence begets violence and blood begets blood, and many will die before the devil has his quota. One can never underestimate the power of retribution.

THE COTTAGE

Men are men until they encounter evil. And after, they are compelled to do evil itself.

Turning their backs on New York, John and Katie Mears purchase their dream home in colonial Connecticut, the place they hope to raise their firstborn and build life as a family. But the cradle of the American nation has a haunting past, and they find themselves swallowed by a dark history, one of blood and anguish, a specter of the country's painful birth in the slaughter of pilgrim times. The dark crucible of the nation is yet manifest. Blood debt is eternal, and sooner or later history calls for retribution. It is the blood of innocents that pays for the sins of the father.

MEAT

In the murky wake of the financial crisis a string of establishments pop up across Europe catering to a hedonistic underground, its clientele beholden to a strange, hallucinatory meat. Stoked by the fleshy and charismatic Hugo and fuelled by voracious consumption of ecstasy, the craze spreads from the heart of Europe all the way to the Mediterranean, where in Athens the financial elite begin to turn on each other. Murder, barbecue and apocalyptic raving ensues, culminating in the most savage party Mykonos has ever seen. Follow the story to its destructive end, where consumption eats itself alive.

NOTES FROM A CANNIBALIST

1847. Assuming the identity of a dead Jesuit priest, a survivor of the famine in Ireland travels to South America where he is tasked with rebuilding the missions among the natives. Inducted into local life, Father James Carmichael finds love with a native woman and becomes acquainted with the ways of the Guaraní, discovering ayahuasca and ritualism. In a battle with his own gods and demons, the priest fights for the life he envisions, his own self the ultimate stake of the struggle. Worlds are shattered, realities crumbled, lives destroyed. His soul victim to the crucible of the New World, what is tempered in the chaos will be outside his control.

A WHORE'S SONG

Hidden away in the backstreets of Amsterdam is a secretive whorehouse, open only to those in the know, where torture, pain and extreme sexual sport are the vehicle to understanding and self-knowledge. Run by the obscure Madame Zhu, the establishment is a magnet to the city's elite and mad soul-seekers alike. Two lives collide in a chaotic downward spiral brought about by psychoactives and sexual torture when, over the course of a day, a whore recounts her life as a destroyer of egos and one man is forced to face his deepest demons. Cast out into the far reaches of his mind, will he make it back from the other side?

In a world where the weak become prey and strength means brutality, living may come at the cost of dying first.

THE BOOK OF GOD

God has lost the plot. He spends his days in the trees killing birds, or crawling through the bushes to watch humans at their rut. His only companion and sole remaining attendant, a withered and tortured scribe, chronicles the Lord's descent into madness as he struggles to bring order to *The Book of Souls*, a record of every being that has ever passed and the reason for the Lord's suffering. But when the Scribe is forced to hire a maid to aid in the care of the Almighty, the introduction of a buxom woman into God's life brings chaos in its wake. Suffering rejection, humiliation and loathing of humankind, God seeks a way to bring back Christ and trigger the Apocalypse.

The Book of God is a work of prose, poetry and black humour that casts an irreverent eye on the holy trinity of sex, death and madness.

Ultan Banan started writing as a way of getting his head straight, discovering in the process that staying busy is the only way to stop oneself going insane. He devotes what time he can to writing, doing his best to avoid gainful employment by increasingly creative means. He lives on the move but dreams of a small cottage on a foul and inhospitable coast somewhere. Currently in Scotland.

Latest news at
ultanbanan.com

Substack:
ultanbanan.substack.com

Twitter:
twitter.com/ultanbanan